THE NEW NEW DELHI BOOK CLUB

THE NEW NEW DELHI BOOK CLUB

RADHIKA SWARUP

Published by Tranquebar, an imprint of Westland Books, a division of Nasadiya Technologies Private Limited, in 2024

No. 269/2B, First Floor, 'Irai Arul', Vimalraj Street, Nethaji Nagar, Alapakkam Main Road, Maduravoyal, Chennai 600095

Westland, the Westland logo, Tranquebar and the Tranquebar logo are the trademarks of Nasadiya Technologies Private Limited, or its affiliates.

ISBN: 9789357768832

10 9 8 7 6 5 4 3 2 1

This is a work of fiction. Names, characters, organisations, places, events and incidents are either products of the author's imagination or used fictitiously.

Typeset by Jojy Philip
Printed at Parksons Graphics Pvt. Ltd

Contents

For Anaia,

my own precious, precocious, impossible Navya

The New New Delhi Book Club

Shami had known about the Singhs moving in next door before they came over to introduce themselves. They were a young couple – the man a clean-shorn Sikh, the woman pretty and quick to smile – but the very night of their arrival was marked by loud howls that splintered his rest. There was no precursor to the noise; no shouting, no slamming of doors, and for Shami, who had just dropped off to sleep, first in his armchair and then, as he woke with a stiff neck, repairing to his bed, the noise had seemed like a pneumatic drill boring into his head.

For a brief moment he had wondered if he was hungover. His drinking, of course, had grown more temperate as he had aged, and he now largely restricted himself to a solitary whisky and soda before dinner, but he knew his trouble lay outdoors the minute the dogs outside began their accompanying cacophony. It was a farrago of noises, all bad-tempered, all rising in hysteria, but Shami slowly identified a new note: the ceaseless crying of a young child.

A delivery truck arrived early the next day. The lady of the house stood issuing polite instructions while dressed in tracksuit bottoms and rubber chappals painted in the colours of the Brazilian flag. She had a soft voice, and when she raised it to attract the attention of the workers, it grew in pitch, a little like the cry of an injured animal. 'Please,' she was saying as she held open the gate to her house, 'the boxes are all marked with the names of the rooms they have to be placed in.'

Shami came out onto the street and tapped her on the shoulder. She started at the contact; a deer caught in the headlights. 'I'm ....' he began, conscious that she might have forgotten their last interaction, but she was starting to unfreeze. She was nodding her head vigorously in memory, she was smiling, she was telling him how nice it was to see him again, and he thought he had better not waste any time on idle pleasantries.

'Was it you who was making all that clatter last night?'

'Yes,' she said, cringing. The men wandered indoors unheeded. 'Or no. It was my child.'

'It woke me up,' he said in a surly voice. 'Woke half the neighbourhood up too, I'm sure.'

'I can imagine,' she said, nodding earnestly as he continued to glower at her. 'I am so sorry. It's just that it was the first time Navya—that's my daughter—slept in her new room. She was frightened, the poor thing.'

'Well.'

The woman held a slender, bangled arm out to him. 'I'm Natasha,' she said, smiling. 'I'm very sorry again about last night. Once we're settled in, I hope you will join me and Jussie for a cup of tea.'

The workers had returned, and they hoisted a new load of boxes on their backs.

'Careful,' Natasha called out. 'The items for the lounge are very fragile.' She turned to follow them indoors, but as she was leaving, she asked Shami, 'There are a few dogs in the house opposite, no?'

'Yes,' Shami said grimly. 'The stupid woman keeps thirty.'

The child cried every night for a week, and every night for a week was joined by a demented canine orchestra. As Shami was taking his morning walk one day during that hellish period, Mrs Khanna from two doors down asked him if he'd been kept up by the noise.

'Yes, damn it,' he said. 'As if the kid wasn't enough, the dogs start up in accompaniment.'

'Waise, the woman herself is nice, Rastogi-ji,' said Mrs Khanna. She wore a magenta velour tracksuit and pumped her arms as she walked, as if she were on a military drill. 'She's taken a few days' leave from work to finalise the move. The child will be left with an ayah once the mother returns to the office.' She stopped, leaned forward and wagged her finger at Shami, her scarlet nail shining. 'I'm telling you, this is why the child keeps crying. No family support.'

Shami shook his head and Mrs Khanna smiled. 'Still, the woman *is* nice. Sent me a beautiful fruit basket after I complained yesterday. Maybe you should complain too and she will send you some fruit to apologise.' This time

Shami laughed. 'Arre, seriously. There was a good lot of loot in there. Guavas, fat pomegranates, grapes and the juiciest mausamis I have ever tasted …'

Shami didn't complain, and no fruit basket was delivered. Mrs Khanna's words had made him consider his fruit consumption though, which had fallen since Suparna's death. He had gorged on the foods she hadn't liked for weeks after her passing—greasy biryanis, seekh kebabs ordered from Chick'n'Fish, deep fried bread pakoras—but after his talk with Mrs Khanna, he thought for the first time about the oranges his wife had been in the habit of ordering in the winter months.

They would sit out on the old coir charpai in the dim sunshine, Suparna peeling each orange, portioning segments, and removing the pith before piling them onto his plate. He would take the first bite carelessly, having forgotten his previous experiences with the fruit, and a dribble of juice would run down his unshaven chin. 'You do this every year!' his wife would hoot. 'Every year you forget how juicy these santras are.'

That day Shami made Chetan, the boy who worked for him, run to the market to fetch him the fruit. The boy returned, and the pair sat on the roof in the early evening—Shami on the charpai he took out of storage, Chetan perching on an ancient mora—while the oranges were peeled. Shami took his first bite, mindful in Suparna's absence to bite into the flesh with care, but there was no escape of orange juice, and all he tasted was the sharp-sweet tang of the fruit. 'The fruits madam picked were sweeter,' he complained.

'She bought from the market further away, sir,' Chetan replied in a soothing voice. 'I'll go there tomorrow morning.'

Shami and Suparna had had one child, a daughter called Ashima who left to study in England when she was eighteen. She had found employment there, married there, and now she raised her children there. He counted himself lucky if she visited once a year. Not that he could blame her. Life got busy, and in those frantic early years of parenting, every moment seemed balanced on the precipice of catastrophe.

The last time they had all descended on them—Ashima and her family—it had felt like a circus was in town. They'd been up from dawn, he and Suparna, babysitting, changing nappies, taking the children out for walks and for illicit ice creams, telling them stories of when the monkey god Hanuman breached the ocean with a single leap. He'd felt like they'd been on an assault course after Ashima and the kids had left to return to their lives, and for a good week afterwards, everything—every toot of the ice cream cart, every burst of childish laughter on the street, every cartoon that appeared on screen as they flicked through channels, every bowl of kheer Chetan produced for the bereft couple—reminded them of what they had lost.

Relations remained formal. Not on Natasha's part; she was always ready with a smile and a greeting when their paths crossed, but Shami continued to be irritated by the child, Navya. She hadn't cried after that initial week, but an inauspicious first impression had been set, and Shami continued to bear a grudge on account of the sleep he had lost.

The girl attended a school nearby, making local friends, and they often met at the house next door for play dates. The children made a lot of noise, screaming, chattering, laughing, throwing balls and breaking earthenware flower pots, which invariably set the dogs in the opposite house off. Shami noticed there was a ten-second lag between the cracking of a flower pot and the first battle cry from across the street, and he took advantage of the interval to disappear deeper into his home.

He grew to understand the child's patterns—her school hours, the nap she took over the hottest hours of the afternoon, her bedtime—and began to adjust for them. He took his morning walk before the child left for school, spent a quiet morning reading and pottering about in the garden, and began to take a siesta around the time Navya did. No alarm clock was required to wake him; Navya's spirited play achieved this more effectively than any alarm could. Shami would slip off to the club for a round of golf as she made merry in her garden.

It was when the country was locked down that Shami next spoke to the Singhs. The phone rang early in the morning, before Shami had had his first cup of tea, and he knew it couldn't be his daughter calling.

He answered the phone. 'Mr Rastogi,' came a breathy voice, 'I got your number from the local directory, and wanted to call to see if you were well.'

'Who is this?'

'Natasha,' said the voice, clearly taken aback by the directness of the question. 'You know, your neighbour?'

'Okay,' came the gruff reply as Shami checked the clock. 'Well, is something the matter?'

'Navya and I were worried about you, all alone at this time. She wanted me to call to let you know that we are here to help in any way we can.'

Shami sighed.

'The store in the market delivers to us. We can add anything you need to our order—vegetables, medicines … just let me know.'

'That won't be necessary,' said Shami. He was conscious he sounded rude and tried to soften his tone. 'I'll be fine. My boy will go to the market when needed.' He didn't offer Chetan's services. 'There's no need for you to worry about me at all.'

Ashima called every day to scold him. Was he eating properly, was he having his multivitamins, had he made sure no one was coming in from outside? 'Yes, baba,' he said, miming ennui. 'The cleaning lady has been paid until the end of next month and told to stay at home. Chetan and I manage on our own.'

'And no going out?'

'When I didn't go out, you told me I needed to exercise, and now that I want to exercise, you tell me to stay at home.'

'Papa! You know you have to be careful.'

With no variety to break up his routine—no morning walks or afternoon golf sessions, no Saturday brunches with his old college friends—there was little to separate one day from the next, and so it could have been a week after Natasha's call, or a fortnight later, that Shami first saw Navya. He had heard her often enough but hadn't yet encountered her in the flesh. She, of course, had ordinarily been busy with her school and her friends, and as he had occupied himself with avoiding her, they hadn't ever come across one another.

It surprised him, then, when as he took a book out to read on his front lawn early one morning, he heard a small voice calling out to him. A throat was cleared, a tiny cough followed, and as Shami jumped up in alarm—was the virus spreading?—a little face peered over the fence. 'Excuse me, Mr Rastogi?' She appeared to be six, maybe seven years old, too young to have reached the railing she gripped on her own, and Shami craned his neck to see if anyone was holding her up. But no, she had climbed up on a rickety wooden ladder, and stood smiling at him, and nodding as if to encourage him to converse. 'I wanted,' she said in an indistinct voice still finding its fluency, 'to see what you look like.'

'Please,' he said. The ground the girl had set the ladder on was uneven, and he worried she would fall over. 'Please,' he said again, as she smiled to see him fret, 'just climb down.'

Navya was undeterred. 'What are you reading?'

He looked at her again and wondered if it was safe to reach out and hold her steady. He decided against it; the risk was too great. 'Please, beta, just climb down.' She looked stubborn in her twin pigtails, a little tyrant like his Ashima had been. 'You'll fall,' he said, his voice rising with his agitation.

She laughed, the little rascal, and he knew she thought no ill could befall her; no spill, no illness, no tears.

'Look,' he now said, looking towards the gate. 'I have an idea.' He pointed towards the entrance. 'How about you climb down and I meet you by your front gate? I'll stand on one side of it and you can stand on the other, so we'll both remain safe.'

This solution pleased the girl, and she began to descend her ladder as Shami stood watching with bated breath.

They met by Navya's front gate, continuing their conversation through the slats between the grills. Navya, more than Shami, made sure he stood far enough away to maintain safety. 'It's best if we don't directly face each other. It's an old person's virus,' she told him without sentimentality. 'If you catch it, you will probably die.'

He was minded to take offence. Had no one taught her manners? Then he saw her looking so solemnly at him that his heart melted. Ashima had worn just such a dress when she was a child—red with white polka dots and a bright satin bow round her waist.

She pointed at him and asked again, 'What are you reading?'

'Oh,' he smiled, lifting the book, 'it's *Malgudi Days*.'

'*Malgudi Days*?'

'Have you heard of it?'

'No,' came the reply.

'You haven't?' he said. 'Why, this is my daughter's copy I'm reading.'

'Daughter?' asked Navya with interest. 'You have a daughter?' And then, before he could respond, 'Mama told me you lived alone.'

'Your Mama's right,' said Shami. 'My daughter is a little older than you. She has a son and a daughter of her own now.'

Navya's attention seemed to have returned to the book in Shami's hand. 'Why are you reading a children's book?'

'Because it's a very wise book,' he said. 'And because reading the books my daughter enjoyed reminds me a little of her.'

'I'd like to read it.'

'Maybe,' he suggested, 'I can lend it to you after lockdown is over.'

The next morning, Natasha called. 'I'm so sorry,' she said, 'But Navya insists she has to talk to you. I tried to hold her off for as long as I could.'

The child came on the phone. 'I have an idea.'

'Good morning, Navya.'

'You know that table you have on your veranda for disinsecting parcels?'

'I do indeed,' he said. 'But how do *you* know about it?'

'Well,' she carried on, swerving his question. 'We have a table like that too. We keep our letters and our deliveries there for three days. Mama tells me the sun helps dis-insect them.'

'Really?'

'Yes,' she asserted. 'So …'

A long pause followed, and Shami enquired encouragingly, 'So?'

'So,' she said, 'when you finish reading your book, maybe you can post it through our letter box.'

'Maybe.'

'And then Mama can put it on the table to dis-insect for three days. We'll have to be careful, of course.'

'Of course.'

'I'll make sure Mama washes her hands thoroughly after she's touched your book.'

'That's very wise.'

'I thought so too.'

The next morning, Shami made the drop. The street was still quiet, still empty of cars and the vendors who usually worked their way around the neighbourhood's lanes, but as the book fell through Navya's letterbox and settled, it made a low sound that put Shami in mind of a coin tossed down the depths of a wishing well.

The following day, Shami received some mail in return. A Roald Dahl book he wasn't familiar with: *Tales of Childhood*. The book was accompanied by a card with instructions in capital letters: MR RASTOGI, THIS IS THE FIRST BOOK YOU ARE READING AS PART OF THE NEW

NEW-DELHI BOOK CLUB. PLEASE WASH YOUR HANDS AFTER PUTTING THE BOOK ON YOUR TABLE. NO READING FOR THREE DAYS.

And then, underneath followed a line in a neat hand: *I find this book boring, but Mama thinks you will like it.*

When he next spoke to Ashima, he asked her if she had read *Tales of Childhood.*

'It's an autobiographical account,' she said. 'I think I've read it but I can't be sure.'

'There's a girl who has moved in next door,' he told her. 'She and I have set up a book club that she calls the New New-Delhi Book Club. I lent her your old copy of *Malgudi Days* and she lent me *Tales of Childhood*.'

A pause followed. Shami considered speaking, when Ashima said, 'I'm glad you're seeking new company, Papa, but I hope you're being careful.'

He laughed. 'The girl,' he pointed out, 'is six years old.'

'Oh.'

'And as much of a bully as you are.'

'But …'

'And,' he added, 'before you scold me again, I am being careful. The little dictator has given me strict instructions. I'm to wash my hands after placing the book on the table to "disinsect", and then I'm not to read it for at least three days.'

She laughed then. A child's voice called out to her from across the line. 'Wait a second, angel,' Ashima called out, and then said to her father, 'I see you're in good hands, Papa.'

'The second-best pair,' he told her. 'The second best.'

This Too Was Love

Sameer and I went to the theatre on the 28th of February this year. We sat, knee by knee, with a thousand or more strangers, breathing the same air—coughing, yawning—laughing at a slapstick moment. We queued at the bar for our overpriced gin and tonics, we wandered through Soho afterwards to find a place with a free table for two, and we filed into the night time Tube to make our way back home to the babysitter, who seemed to have developed a cough as the evening had progressed.

For ages, I had felt like Cassandra, cursed with a foresight no one would credit. As it had all begun; the news stories, the desperate situation in China, tragic but distant, and then as it had moved closer to home, to Europe, to a familiar culture where everyone lived and loved as we lived and loved; dining out, commuting to work and drinking with their meals, so many had continued to think that it wouldn't impact them.

I began to work from home and told Sameer to do the same, but he told me I was being paranoid. 'Flights come in from Wuhan every day,' he said, as if that was reason to abandon caution. 'Let's face it, the virus is already in circulation.'

'So we just sit back and wait to fall ill?'

'No,' he said, 'we take precautions. We avoid rush-hour travel. We avoid crowded places.' He looked at me and ran his fingers across my forehead, as if to ease away my worry. 'But life can't stop either, Ashima.'

He was convincing, but he continued to run late at the office, travelling back when the Tube was at its most crowded, where, he told me, they all jumped in unison if someone in their carriage coughed. He'd return home tired, and for all his talk about being careful, he routinely forgot to wash his hands or rotate his coats to avoid infection.

Mihir's school was planning their annual concert for the beginning of March, and as I and a few of the other mothers—it was always the women—voiced our concerns, we were assured in the politest way possible that there was no need to panic. The scientists in charge were monitoring the news, and they would tell the schools to shut down if there was any need for it. I could have laughed; I could have cried. It was the women who panicked; it was the men who prepared. Only this time the men in charge saw no reason to prepare.

In India, it was Niharika who kept me updated. She had remained in the neighbourhood as the rest of us had moved for love or for work, and it was she who now told me that the Sikh grocer in the local market had set up a delivery service. 'I pay him online,' she explained, 'and if you want, I can pay for Shami uncle too. We can settle accounts later.'

I relayed the offer to Papa, who told me I was worrying needlessly. Everything was in hand. I asked him if he had stocked up on supplies. He laughed in reply, his tone indulgent, as if I was the one being unreasonable. 'Arre bhai,' he told me, 'I have everything I need. Chetan goes daily for fresh supplies.'

'People are stocking up,' I told him. 'I know they've run out of Maggi noodles in the market.'

'Maggi noodles.' He sniffed, still impossible, still cavalier. 'That's children's food.'

'There's a woman,' I replied, 'a friend of a friend, who has purchased 20 kilos of rice and 20 kilos of wheat flour to prepare for lockdown.'

'Don't fret,' he said in a calm voice, and I recalled the tone he used to employ anytime I had worried about revising for my exams at school. 'Don't worry,' he said, half whispering, half crooning down the phone, 'It'll all be fine.'

I could almost hurl the phone across the room. He never took anything seriously, but then, he had never had to. It was Ma who had nagged me into an education, and Ma who organised things so seamlessly that clouds never appeared on Papa's horizon.

'Maybe,' I said, trying not to show my frustration, 'you could look at powdered milk …'

'Now you're being kooky,' he said, turning to the word he had used in my childhood. 'If the girl doesn't study,' Ma would threaten whenever I tired of revising, addressing Papa as if I wasn't present, 'she'll be cooking in someone else's kitchen all her life.' The predictions would grow progressively dire. 'She'll work in a salon waxing the hair off a fat sethani's thighs. She'll be selling glass bangles in the market.' At that point, Papa and I would dissolve into helpless giggles. 'You're being kooky,' he would tell her, as if to tease her from scolding.

'You're being kooky,' Papa was saying again, trying to lift me from my worry, and then, as I relented, 'There's no need for all this powdered milk rubbish. I will continue to consume fresh cow's milk from Mother Dairy as I always have.'

The deaths mounted. They were dying in the hundreds in the northern tip of a country so dedicated to beauty that it seemed as if art was everywhere, in the shop, in the fountains, in the winding lanes of its ancient towns, in the open arms of St Peter's Basilica, in the altar pieces in its cool, dark churches, and I found myself saying to Sameer, 'But how can they lose 800 people? How can a region that size lose 800 people in a day?'

The toilet flooded in Mihir's school the week before lockdown. It was fixed, but the water pressure remained indifferent, so the boys either didn't wash their hands after using the toilet, or walked up a floor, their dirty hands trailing on the banisters, to where the hand sanitiser dispensers were. I bought him bottles of hand sanitiser, first at £1.50 from Boots, and then, as supply started running low, at £12.50 from the local pharmacy. But his friends always asked him for some, and my poor happy, complying child would return home from school with an empty bottle of the magic rub.

I hadn't been to India since Ma's passing last summer, and that time, Sameer had handled the children while I had flown back. We had thought to travel at the end of March to time it with the children's Easter holidays. But then, lockdown was announced in India before it was in the UK, announced almost before a single case was registered. Suddenly we were unwelcome in our own country. In the beginning, the measures weren't overly stringent; new arrivals were only subjected to a quarantine, and though Papa argued that we should travel, and that we could all quarantine together, a new diktat announcing that people of Indian origin were no longer welcome in India brought an end to all debates. We were suddenly the pariahs, those of us in the West, we were now the disease-ridden refugees from a backward country. Sameer and I had retained our Indian passports, but Mihir and Nikki were British, and we now faced the prospect of being allowed into the country while our children were turned back, and after the first shock of the announcement had passed, I saw it was for the best. There would be no telling Papa not to hug the children, and no telling him not to pepper their faces with a hundred kisses, and this enforced separation seemed the best way I knew to keep him safe.

Lockdown was finally announced in the UK; I no longer had to worry about Sameer commuting into work and no longer had to worry about the kids at school. I no longer had to think of stocking up on hand sanitiser for Mihir.

Things ran out in the shops, and for months, we couldn't get a supermarket delivery slot. There was no pasta in stock, and then no flour as people turned to baking bread at home. Sourdough starters became the new prized commodity, and I counted myself lucky that I had a friend who could guide me if I did need to take to baking my own loaves. Food Armageddon to accompany all that the virus had visited upon us.

And yet, I was happy at home. Sameer suffered from cabin fever at times, inventing excuses to run out for a cup of coffee or a bottle of milk, but the threat of contagion was largely limited. For weeks the worry had been building, the concerns about Italy, the matches that were allowed to go ahead in England itself, the conferences, the plays, the concerts. It had all seemed careless, and as I saw the rest of the world wake to the threat of the virus, as I saw the rest of the world close borders and shut schools and offices, and as I saw my father tell me to not fret, my own anxiety levels shot up.

Everything domestic had always been in Mama's care. The household budget, the savings for my education and marriage. She decided if we could afford to go on holiday or if we were restricted to visiting family during my summer break. She decided if I could get a new skirt for the new school year, or if she had to let down the hem of my old one. Papa's clothes too—his shirts and trousers and smalls—were all purchased by her, such that he never noticed anything running out. She was in charge of his food and his favourite snacks and his vitamins, and of his bottles of Johnny Walker too, which she would often tell me to purchase from the airport duty-free shop on my annual visits.

I spoke to him daily now, worrying he would stop listening if I nagged too much, and largely, I gave him our news; information about Mihir's progress with virtual schooling, my attempts to make sure Nikki learned her multiplication tables. It seemed to me that he wasn't taking the situation seriously though, and when I would ask him if he was taking care to eat well, he would complain. 'How long can I stay indoors?'

'Papa …'

I would picture him setting his jaw across the phone. 'This is not sustainable.'

'It's not forever,' I told him. 'A month or two, maybe? And you're lucky, your lockdown coincides with India's worst months for weather. Mine coincides with London's best. We've had a horrid winter too, don't forget, with storms hitting us all February, and I would like nothing better than to go out in the sunshine.'

He still complained, talking about wanting to play golf in the evenings, telling me isolation wasn't good for his mental health. I had to smother my disbelief. Mental health. Mental health? Where had he even heard of the phrase? When had he turned so precious about his feelings?

I told him I wanted to talk to Chetan to make sure he was behaving, and he told me I was treating him like a baby. 'You can't do this,' he said even as he handed the phone over to Chetan. I heard him by Chetan the whole time I spoke, telling him not to listen to me, that I was a bully, that I was mistreating him, and I knew he had put me on speakerphone so nothing could escape him. I made Chetan agree to the precautions that were needed, but I knew they were rolling their eyes as I spoke, gesturing and signalling to each other that I was over-reacting.

After Chetan was off the phone, Papa continued to tell me I was infantilising him. He complained so incessantly and with such animation that it would take me a while to realise that this was contact too, this back and forth between father and daughter, this tug and pull of exasperation and affection.

It took me a while to realise that this too was love.

Saloni Coughs

'Just come home,' Ma cried into his ear every evening. 'I don't care how you do it, just come back from that godless, disease-ridden place.'

'How can I, Ma?' Chetan would try to reason with her, whispering even though he knew his voice wouldn't carry to the old man. 'No trains are running. No buses are, either. Do you want me to walk like those poor labourers who have lost everything?'

'What lost everything?' she would shoot back. 'They're returning to their families, to their home. We are your family, not that old man you work for day and night.'

'You don't know what you are saying, Ma. Those people didn't have a choice.' He paused, taking care to speak calmly. 'Their employers stopped feeding them. They had nothing; no food to give their families, no way to survive … Even now, as they walk thousands of kilometres in this heat, they have to rely on the charity of strangers to live. Maybe a chai-wallah will give them a few biscuits or a passing car will give them some water, but it's a miserable situation.'

'I don't know, I just want you home.'

'Think, Ma, please,' he said. 'The old man treats me well and he pays me well. It is his money that keeps the household running back home.'

'It's *your* hard-earned money,' she shot back, but he heard her waver.

'The work here is simple, and I only have one person to run after. I have a roof over my head, I eat well—the same food the old man does—chicken, mutton … you name it. And you're asking me to come home at this uncertain time? Who knows how much worse the situation could get.'

She didn't argue then, and Chetan breathed a sigh of relief. It was true, what he said to her, but what he hadn't told her was that there was another reason to stay on in Delhi. Saloni had finally agreed to talk to him after months of trying. She was standoffish as a rule, taking on the airs of her mistress, who appeared on a TV show once a week. He had memorised her patterns—when she left her rooftop room to go down into the house for her duties, when she went out to the market, and even when she went into the little lean-to bathroom next to her room to do her business. He especially waited for the days she washed her hair. Before she would coil the still-damp strands into a bun, he would catch a glimpse of her hair falling thick and soft on her kurta with all the promise of the night.

He thought she hadn't noticed him observing her from his own rooftop opposite hers, but one day, as he stood waiting behind her at the line outside Mother Dairy, she whipped around and looked him straight in the eye. Chetan was too taken aback but he nodded as she asked him to stop watching her. 'Stalking,' she said. 'Stock-king.' The word was unfamiliar to Chetan, but Mahesh from across the street later told him that it meant he was troubling her. 'Troubling her?' he asked. 'I've never even spoken to her.'

'Arre, so what? Just google it and you'll see,' Mahesh said, shaking his head knowledgably.

Google told Chetan the word meant he was following her, but here too he frowned. He hadn't once done that. He had changed his hour for going to the market to chime with hers, but at every point he'd kept a respectful distance, not looking in her direction, trying not to casually brush past her. And he had varied his routine, arriving before her one day and leaving after her on another to avoid making her uncomfortable. And for her to have accused him of stalking!

Chetan stopped keeping time with Saloni. He purchased all his supplies in the mornings, going to the market after serving sir his morning tea and biscuits, and if they ran out of an ingredient, it got added to the following morning's shopping list. Shami sir was easy-going, thank heavens, and didn't complain if there were no green chillies with his lunch or if the tadka in the daal was less tangy than he was used to.

He didn't see Saloni for a month or more. The boys he met on his rounds to the market—Mahesh, Bahadur and Veer—found him surly and uncommunicative, and teased that he was wasting away for the love of Saloni, but he insisted that he had forgotten all about her.

But then, one morning six or seven weeks after he had stopped syncing his plans with hers, he stepped out of the house to find her waiting. He checked his watch. It was still before eight in the morning, the time for her to have her shower. It was Tuesday too, when she normally washed her hair, and as he looked at her, he thought he glimpsed a dewy dampness at the base of her throat.

He turned from her, walking swiftly towards the market.

'Today,' she said, so softly that he slowed down. 'Today I am stalking you.'

'Where did you learn such a heavyweight English word?'

He expected her to say she had been educated at school to a level that took her even further out of his reach, but she smiled sheepishly. 'My madam, you know. She had some trouble with a man who wouldn't leave her alone and I would hear her say that word when she spoke to her friends or the police.'

'Hai bhagwan,' he said, tugging at his earlobes. 'Are you going to call the police to arrest me now?'

'No,' she replied in a coy voice, 'and I hope you don't call the police to arrest me.'

That was before the sudden lockdown. They hadn't met since. Shami sir was more careful than Saloni's ma'am on account of his age, but his worries were compounded by those of Ashima didi. She called from England and had her father put Chetan on the line. 'Papa never listens,' she complained, 'but I want you to make sure he takes care.'

'Of course, didi.'

'No going out for him. No golf, no drinks with friends.'

'No, didi.'

'And no letting in anyone from outside either.'

'No, didi.'

'And who comes to clean the house these days? Ask her to stop coming immediately.'

Chetan informed Ashima that since public transport wasn't running, they had paid Purnima, their cleaner, and asked her to stay at home. He'd felt a stab of envy as he'd counted out the notes to give to the woman the last time she had cleaned. She had received a month and a half's pay just to sit still, and there he was, working harder to pick up the slack on the same money he always made.

'And what are you doing with the mail you receive?'

'Mail?'

'Letters. Papa still receives letters, doesn't he?'

Chetan nodded, then realised she wouldn't be able to see his reaction. 'Yes, didi.'

'And all those Amazon parcels Papa is so fond of ordering. What do you do with those?'

'We … we are very careful, didi.'

She sighed. 'Just as I thought. I want you to put a table in the veranda outside. Do you understand me, Chetan?'

He nodded again, then hurried to speak. 'Yes, didi.'

'Do you still have that old table that was kept in the kitchen?'

'Yes, didi.'

'Good,' she replied. 'That should be the right size. Now I want you to take it out onto the veranda, and anytime any parcels come, I want you to put them out there for three days before you take them inside.'

Chetan had questions. 'But didi, the wood will rot in the sun. And what if someone steals the parcels?'

Ashima laughed. 'I'll buy you a new table after all of this is over if I have to. And if anyone wants to open our gate and venture into the veranda to steal an Amazon parcel, they must be more desperate than the rest of India is at this time.'

Weeks passed and Chetan's trips to the market grew scarce and then stopped. Shami Sir called the grocer, who began to deliver the household's shopping to the doorstep.

'Do I need to pay the delivery boy?' Chetan asked.

'No,' the old man replied. 'The shopkeeper will add the bill to my account, and he says we can settle it once all of this is over.'

'Yes, sir,' replied Chetan. 'Or when things ease up, I can go and pay the balance in cash as well.'

It was something, it was hope, it was a plan, it was an excuse to pass in front of Saloni's house as he took the long way to the market. It was a text message sent to her to stand outside her gate so they could exchange a brief word, or if the world still stood after all this passed, it was an ice cream—a cola bar, a chocobar, a mango duet—bought to be presented to her while she pretended she didn't want anything from him.

Her routine, he knew, hadn't changed apart from her visits to the market. She still woke up at roughly the same time, still bathed and fixed her hair before descending into the house for her duties. She still climbed up to use the toilet when the need arose, but after her slur, he hadn't looked out towards her rooftop. 'Stock-ker,' she had called him. The word still stung.

Late one night, she sent him a text message. *I never see you now.*

He typed out one word in reply: *Lockdown.*

Are you in your room?

He considered his response. Her question excited in him the thought of her presence. Was she still working, or had she too retired for the night? Was she in her room on the roof, open to the elements save for one flimsy wooden panel? Was she there, within sight, breathing the same air as he was?

Well?

Yes, I am.

I'm on the roof too, she typed.

He turned his light off, not knowing how to respond, when she shot over another salvo, *'But I think you've gone to sleep.'*

No, I haven't!

You turned the light off.

Chetan quickly switched it back on, watching as the bald bulb burst into light.

That's better.

Aren't you going to bed? he asked, suddenly feeling shy.

No, she wrote back, and then, *It's so pleasant right now*.

Chetan rose from his bed, straightening out his pyjama-kurta as he walked out onto the roof. The night was dark, but he saw a light shining on her rooftop.

His phone buzzed. *Turn the torch on*.

He looked up, but couldn't see her. He thought he could make out an indistinct shape move in the terrace across, but couldn't be certain. It was too dark. Chetan looked back at the message on his phone, when he saw a torch light being shone in his direction. His phone buzzed again. *The torch light! On your home screen*.

He'd used the torch on his phone a few times when the electricity had gone off, but never up here, and never out in the open. He turned it on now, marvelling as an alien world opened up to him. The roof at night, so silent, so cool. He felt the wind pick up and saw the marigolds Suparna ma'am had planted swaying in flowerpots on the roof. He looked across and Saloni—that indistinct shape he had spied—grew firm in front of him. She wore a diaphanous cloth that blew in the breeze, a hand-me-down from her employer, perhaps. She wore her hair loose, and though he couldn't be sure, he thought it fell all the way down to her waist. He couldn't see her clearly, couldn't make out her features or see if her nose pin sparkled under the moon's gentle light, but he knew she was smiling at him. The night grew fragrant with the smell of raat ki rani, and he grinned inanely, not sure how their interaction could progress, not wanting it to end, when he felt his phone ping.

Well?

He thought hard. She had called him a 'stock-ker', but then again, it was she who had lured him out. *I wish I could leap over our roofs and reach you.*

There was no reply.

Chetan looked across and saw Saloni had turned her back to him. He turned off his torch and stepped miserably back from the balcony railing, certain he'd been too forward. She had taken offence.

He turned his phone up to see if a message had flashed, but the screen remained dark. This was it, the end. All his hard work undone in one unthinking moment. He heard a quiet sound; a whisper, a sob, and he was sure he had caused her grief. She thought him a creep. She had used the word 'stock-ker' in high-spirited jest, but now he'd proven her right.

He wrung his hands hopelessly. He didn't look across at her terrace, and considered retreating to his room, when there was a buzzing noise from his phone. There was a blinding burst of light, bringing with it the notification of a voice note.

He didn't dare listen. He did turn on his torch, looking to take his cue from Saloni. It all depended on her; despair or hope.

She didn't smile.

She had her hand on her hip, but she inclined her head slightly, and he pressed play.

It was a two-word reply delivered in a disapproving voice: *Shoshal distansing*, and as he looked up slack jawed, she turned and sauntered mercilessly off to her rest.

They met every evening as Delhi grew cool. Chetan ached through the day to see her, wondering if she was outdoors as he went to put Shami sir's mail away, or if she took a rest in the hottest hours of the afternoon after serving her employer lunch, but he feared she would take offence if he suggested a rendezvous. She dictated their meetings, shining a light onto his roof when she wished to interact. He retired to bed earlier now, yawning as Shami sir ate his dinner, stretching his arms out in mimed exhaustion until the old man told him to go to sleep. He would rush up, keeping his door open so that the minute she showed any willingness, he could trip out, his phone held aloft to shine his way to their assignation.

By now he knew that she always wore her hair loose when not working, and took pride in its full, straight length. She was always in a shapeless nightie that was in itself unexciting, but gave him an impression of her body—of her legs, her buttocks, of the swell of her breasts—as the wind blew. Their interaction was mostly in the shadows, for all the torches blazing across Delhi's rooftops; reactions to a text gauged by the pauses as much as by physical replies. The rare voice notes, to be replayed later and savoured. Their love grew sweeter, felt more tantalising for all the contact they withheld. They never touched, never breathed on the other's upturned flesh, never learnt the contours of the other's face or body, but it was all understood, all taken on promise, like a yellowing mango left untouched on the branch until its tartness intensified and then mellowed, until its fragrance filled the air, and until its fullness, so sweet now, so ephemerally perfect, and so close to spoiling, grew to feel unbearable.

He couldn't sleep at night for thinking of her. He thought he heard her turn in her sleep; he thought he heard her open her door in the mornings to look across at his terrace. He had never been within touching distance of her, but now he imagined he smelt her fragrance, a heady, musty-sweet scent combining the smells of the raat ki rani and the tart secrets of a mango ripening on the stem.

One evening, Shami sir expressed a desire to go up to the terrace. Chetan duly walked him up there, dragging out the old charpai as sir drank his whisky and soda.

'This is a nice spot,' he told Chetan. 'It feels pleasant after staying indoors all day.'

'Yes, sir.'

'Maybe you should sleep out here sometimes,' Shami suggested. 'I'm sure it's more pleasant than your concrete room.'

'No, no, sir,' spoke the boy with puritan modesty. 'Anyone can see.'

Chetan thought he saw Saloni appear on her rooftop. He thought he saw her peer at the pair and the charpai, and he hoped she wouldn't try to distract him. There was an impishness to her that he adored, but it wouldn't do for sir to spot her and consider Chetan's presence on the terrace at night inappropriate. He turned towards her balcony and made a stern face, lifting a finger to his lips before moving studiously back to Shami sir. He thought he heard her cough, once and then again, with surprise or to attract attention, he couldn't be sure. Shami sir detected the sound too as he jumped a little and spilt his drink. Chetan ran to him with a napkin and proceeded to dab at the old man's trousers. A faint cough was heard again.

'These are strange times,' said his employer, 'when an imagined cough can disturb your equilibrium so much.'

'It's alright, sir. I am sure it was nothing.'

There was another sound from her rooftop, and Chetan knew she was determined to attract his attention.

'But you heard it too, didn't you?'

Chetan paused to consider. The air was still now, and Delhi completely silent. The dogs from the opposite house slept, and the noise of children's laughter, such a staple on an early summer evening, was nowhere to be heard. Nothing moved, not the trees, not a car, not a street vendor's cart. 'No, sir,' he told his waiting employer, 'I didn't hear a thing.'

Other Deities

It rained overnight. Rain, she called it, but it had been torrential, whole sheets of glass falling against her roof, and Smita thought back to the time when Om was alive. They would snuggle under the covers when the weather turned like this, and invariably, no matter how much they aged, no matter how much else they ate and saw and experienced, an unexpected downpour would always transport her husband to his childhood.

'It's malpura weather,' he would tell her, recalling the sweet, crisp, deep-fried disks his mother always fed him when it rained. Smita would grumble then, telling him her mother had prepared the treat for her too when it rained, that it had been an excuse for her too to be petted and indulged, but he would pout, looking so much like a spoilt child that she would give in with a laugh. The rain would lash down on them, and she would rise and prepare him the snack that he always associated with a turn in the weather.

She saw the pothole in the road outside her home fill with water. This would be sure to cause chaos, even with the fall in traffic. Smita sighed.

Still, she thought, the rain would bring relief. The temperature had risen to 45 degrees a week ago, and there had been no going out during the day, not even as far as the front door to catch a sign of outside life. Everything had come to a standstill, of course, but once in a while, as Smita came out to retrieve her clothes from the presswallah, she did hear snatches of life. She heard Mrs Bose in conversation with her daughter-in-law. She saw that child next door, the Singh girl, chat with Shami Rastogi, and if he was facing the right way, he would pause in his conversation with the girl and wave to her. He would come over to her gate and they would exchange a few lockdown pleasantries—questions about how they were coping and about how their distant loved ones were faring.

And the boys did call, of course, making sure she wasn't running out of supplies, but they were far away and busy with their own lives. What was it that people said? *A son is a son until he takes a wife but a daughter is a daughter for life.* How Smita had pooh-poohed the others when they had teased her.

She had scoffed, she had laughed, she had told them all—friends, relatives, neighbours—that they were different, her two boys, that they were sensitive and caring. And yet it had been all but immediate, the turn of adoration away from her and to the women they fell in love with, as if they were devotees, her boys, and two deities couldn't co-exist in their pantheons.

Smita looked out of her bedroom window. There was no one to make malpure for now, no one to nag her, and no one to plead and tug at her covers until she grumbled and rose to prepare the batter of sugary, syrupy goodness that always followed rain.

The sky remained dark outside, even though it was nearing eight in the morning. There was no point lazing around; she would have to get up. Smita had a sudden desire for a crisp, steaming hot malpura, and though she would never be able to finish more than a couple of the disks, and though the rest of the batter would almost certainly be thrown away, she knew she wasn't going to be able to resist her urge.

The bedsheet was carefully folded and placed at the end of the bed. The bed itself was patted down, as it had been every morning since her wedding day. The dhoop was moulded into shape, a little like raw clay, a little like the children she had taught to study and to love and to be faithful, and once her morning prayer was completed, Smita walked towards the kitchen.

She didn't turn the lights on despite the grayness of the day. She had grown miserly in unexpected ways since Om's death. Lights wouldn't be switched on unless her eyes ached. If the tea went cold, it would be drunk that way instead of being reheated in the microwave. And now that the cooking girl wasn't coming in, Smita would cook in batches every couple of days to save on the effort and the washing, stretching the same food out over several meals.

She didn't show her quirks to visitors, bathing the home in light when anyone came over, cooking up a storm so that every meal had variety, but when she was on her own, she didn't see the sense in making such a fuss.

It was the lack of light, perhaps, that made her lose her footing. Her long night dress bunched up between her legs, and before she could reach a hand out to steady herself, she felt herself fall across the hard marble of the floor between her room and the kitchen. She heard a sound, a crack, like the snapping of a chicken bone in her mouth, and a sharp pain radiated up her left leg. She put her hand out, felt where it had grazed against the door, and brought it up to view. She would have to bathe it and disinfect it. There would be some Savlon in the kitchen and some gauze too, if she was lucky. Her leg throbbed, pulsing with her breath, and then faster, and warmer, and warmer still, until she felt her throat go parched, until she looked up at the ceiling fan and imagined that it moved.

She must have passed out from her pain, for Smita remembered waking up with parched lips. For a fleet, blessed instant, she forgot about her injury, and instead, she wondered why she found herself on the floor. Then she tried to rise and cried out in pain. It came back to her; the rain, the urge for malpure, the hurry to get to the kitchen, and then the slow-motion tumble on the floor.

Smita tried once more to move, but the pain was excruciating. She put a hand gingerly on her knee, but her skin felt hot and swollen, and she knew it was best not to disturb the area. She tried to drag herself slowly to the phone in her bedroom, but the effort was too great. Her palm was raw from when she had held it out to break her fall, and as she tried to lever herself up on her hands, she found it all hurt; her hands, her shoulders, her hips and her broken leg.

The rain was still belting down, enveloping her thoughts, and though she called out for help, hoping one of her next-door neighbours would break into her home despite all the worries of germs and infection, no one could hear her over the clamour. No one came.

She moved onto her back and stared at the ceiling. Her leg burned red hot. She remained laying on the cold floor, examining her palm and listening to rain lashing against her roof as she tried to ignore the pain. There had been a leak a few years back, with bucket loads of rain water tearing into their living room and staining the walls and the ceiling. How they had scrambled, she and Om, as they heard the water burst in one night, how they had fetched buckets and mops and rushed to clean away the water even as the deluge intensified. Om had brought workmen in the very next morning, and they had sealed the breach. It hadn't leaked since, and Smita had all but forgotten about that night-time drama, but she saw now that it had been a little above where she lay, a little to the right of the fan, and as she looked up, she imagined she saw a crack in the plaster.

With any luck, the seal would hold, and no leak would develop this time. With any luck, the rain would stop. With any luck, they would hear her cry out, a neighbour, a passer-by, a child or Shami Rastogi, and offer her assistance. With any luck, the pain would abate. With any luck, it wouldn't be a fracture and she would be able to drag herself to the phone.

And they would call, her two boys, if not immediately then in a while, in a day or two at the most, the children she had so filled with the ideals of fidelity and constancy that they would think of her even if they now worshipped at the altar of other deities.

Leopard Spotting in Delhi

Cook, clean, wash, repeat—this is how she spent her days now. All day, every day. No one had entered the flat since the lockdown was announced. Not a friend, not a neighbour, not Devi, her capable, stolid much-missed cleaning *wali*.

Jussie locked himself in his office early in the mornings, emerging only for refills of coffee. 'You make the best coffee,' he said to her. 'I don't miss the rubbish they serve at Café Coffee Day.'

'It's just the machine,' she told him. 'You could make it yourself. Maybe make me a cup too one morning.'

'Bah,' he answered. 'I wouldn't know how to figure out that contraption. Just face it, Tasha, no one makes it like you do.'

When they had first moved into the area, they had put out a table and chair set on the veranda overlooking the front lawn. Natasha had purchased it from Flipkart after visiting several showrooms on MG Road. 'We can sit here in the evenings, while Navya plays in the garden. Maybe even invite our neighbours over?' Natasha looked at Jussie, but he was on his phone, typing furiously, sending an email off to work. 'What do you think?' she asked, hating the plaintive note in her voice, but he didn't look up. 'Hmm,' he murmured as if agreeing with whatever she suggested, and Natasha cleared her throat. 'You're never off that thing.'

'What can I do, darling?' he said. 'My work doesn't stop.' He put his phone in his pocket and gave Natasha a peck on the cheek.

'He looks lonely, Jussie.'

'Who?'

'The old man next door.' She pointed at Mr Rastogi's house. 'Maybe we can invite him over one evening. It may be good for Navya. You know how far she is from all her grandparents …'

An invite was duly issued to her neighbour, but no date was set for the visit as the old man responded to her overtures gruffly. Natasha wondered if she had offended him. Perhaps the movers had broken one of his flower pots? She did think to ask, but Mr Rastogi never stopped for long enough for Natasha to pose her awkward question, and in any case, she and Jussie never seemed to have the time to so much as sit outside together either.

An old school friend, Shivani, had turned seer. She filled her home and social media feeds with crystals, and as Coronavirus spread, she began to send daily emails filled with inspirational messages. Natasha didn't remember signing up for the mail-outs, but she skimmed through them as they came through each morning. Most of the messaging was lightly constructive; much of the strife they were going through, as a society, as a family unit, came from negative energy. The negativity blocked progress. Though Natasha mostly mocked the newsletters, reading out to Jussie the choicest claims ascribing the pandemic to bad chakras, she would linger over the final paragraphs of Shivani's emails, where she laid out all she was grateful for.

'What are you grateful for?' her emails would end, and Natasha would close her eyes in contemplation. She was safe; her parents remained healthy, and though her job at the travel agency was unlikely to survive, she had Jussie and Navya with her. 'We're spending more time together,' Shivani wrote. 'In some ways, it feels like our second honeymoon. My husband now notices when I wear a new outfit. He notices when I try out a new hairstyle. I find we are making the most of our time together before life intrudes again, and I hope all of you are too.'

But as Natasha had discovered, Jussie's lockdown only made him busier. Initially she saw this as a good sign. Others were planning for redundancies, and if Jussie was busy, it meant his employment was secure. But then she saw how he rose earlier, forgetting to eat his meals or to shave, forgetting to read Navya her bedtime story as he worked through the evening. His sleep became lighter too; she found that the slightest disturbance—a movement from her, a dog's bark, or a car turning in the street—would rouse him and he would be unable to return to sleep. He didn't tell her he was worried, even as she saw his hair whiten by his temples, even as she saw his laughter lines deepen, and instead of telling him not to stress, she concentrated on lightening his load.

She never asked him to help out around the house, never told him to help Navya with Maths, never complained about the crusty neighbours—not about Mr Rastogi, not about Mrs Khanna next door and not about the woman opposite with her army of dogs. When they sat down in front of the television at the end of the day, she didn't stop him from turning on the superhero movies he never seemed to outgrow.

'Focus on all you are grateful for,' Shivani wrote, and Natasha told herself she was doing just that.

She found her time with Navya to be her greatest joy, and in those early days when they had been too scared to even venture out of their house, when they hadn't yet built up the courage to visit the playground Navya had fallen in love with or to stand outside the child's new friend's house and chat, she and her daughter had found routine helped them occupy themselves.

Thus, the daily sudoku and the daily jigsaw puzzle. And thus, the ritual of the handwash. Once a day Natasha would bring in the parcels of mail she had quarantined on the table in the lawn, and after she came indoors, Navya would stand next to her mother as she washed her hands. The girl would sing out Happy Birthday to time twenty seconds, and only after that, after Natasha's hands had been sufficiently lathered and every centimetre—her nails, her fingers, her thumbs, the webbing between her fingers, her wrists and the lower parts of her forearms—had been scrubbed clean, would Navya let her stop. Natasha complained her hands were growing dry from the repeated handwashing, and Navya brought out a tube of hand cream. She would apply it on her mother's hands, repeating the procedure of the handwash, making sure all was covered, nails and fingers and thumbs and the webbing between fingers and wrists and the lower parts of her arms. Natasha called her Ya-ma; her own little precious, precocious, positive girl-mother.

Delhi continued to hibernate as summer advanced. 'It's just like those chooi-mooi leaves, Mama,' Navya said when Natasha tried to tell her that they would not be going out for a few weeks. There had been some excitement at school about the unexpected holiday, but some of the children had worried that the germs they carried would kill their parents or grandparents. Natasha had assured Navya that they were safe, and that everyone they loved was safe too, but that to make sure everyone remained healthy, they would have to keep their distance from the outside world.

Navya would have to stay away from school and no friends would be able to visit her for a while. 'They do the same too, don't they, those leaves?' Navya had said to her. 'They shrivel into themselves whenever anyone tries to touch them.'

Together, mother and daughter enquired after their neighbours. They called the old man next door to make sure he was safe. Even though she was a newcomer, Natasha had established a good working relationship with the Sikh grocer, who hailed from the same industrial town in Punjab as she did. She offered to add the old man's groceries to her order, but he rebuffed the offer, telling Natasha he had someone to run errands for him, and though Natasha repeated her offer of help, she wondered why her show of goodwill wasn't reciprocated.

Natasha tried to call the lady next door, Mrs Khanna, but the call went unanswered. She had spoken to her once and discovered that she had sons living elsewhere, and Natasha assumed she had left to spend lockdown with them. One evening, she posted a note through the letterbox of the Bose family upstairs, asking them if they needed any help. She hadn't interacted with Mahima, the daughter-in-law, save for a few hurried exchanges at the front gate, but there had been something—their laughing together at one of Navya's jokes, a simultaneous tut at a dog's bark—that had convinced her there could be camaraderie between them. Natasha had mentioned meeting for a drink one evening, and though Mahima had seemed keen, nothing further had been discussed, and then the news had broken and Delhi had retreated into itself. The note, Natasha thought, represented a renewal of amity, and though she told herself she didn't expect a reply, she looked out for a note under her front door every day.

She never received a reply. She told herself the silence didn't bother her, that the Bose family could have missed the note in the rush of cleaning and quarantining that first accompanied lockdown, but late one night as Jussie and she readied themselves for bed, Natasha mentioned her offer to her husband. He tutted. 'You never should have written the note.'

'What have I done wrong? I mean, if anything, it's the Boses who are being rude.'

'They are,' he agreed. 'But I don't like you getting hurt.'

As the noise of Delhi died down, they noticed new sounds. The koyal sang early in the morning, and they read in the papers that a leopard had wandered into a garden in Chandigarh. Navya began to wake early to watch out for a similar incursion in Delhi, but no big cat made an appearance on their lawn. The child continued hopeful, but they saw nothing, no monkey wandering in from the ruins of an abandoned temple, no nilgai strolling in the lane outside, no stray cat even—nothing more exotic than the common sparrow, who Navya laid bread out for each morning.

There was less road noise, which was welcome, though the relative calm did nothing to quieten the dogs in the house opposite. Natasha had gone across the road to introduce herself when they had first moved into the flat. The lady of the house, a tall, hoarse-voiced woman who went by the name of Sunny, had nodded briskly when Natasha pointed to where they lived. She had stood at the gate, not inviting Natasha into her home, nor letting her into the driveway. Natasha had heard a bark, and looked down to see two biggish dogs, about the size of Alsatians, straining against Sunny's hands.

'How many do you have?' Natasha asked, pointing at the dogs. There was further noise from within the property.

'At the moment,' said the woman, 'I have twenty-eight.'

'Wow.'

'I came here with four,' Sunny added, 'and I've rescued the rest.'

Mrs Khanna had warned Natasha off complaining. 'The entire neighbourhood is sick and tired of this Sunny. We've had no peace since she's moved in. But you try and reason with her, and she waves a letter from Maneka Gandhi.' Natasha's eyes had widened, and Mrs Khanna explained, 'The dog lover in parliament. Used to be married to Indira Gandhi's son.'

'I know.'

'The one whose plane crashed, remember?' Mrs Khanna went on, savagely. 'But maybe he's better off where he is. At least he can sleep in peace,' she laughed at her off-colour joke. 'But seriously, *Beta*, we've tried everything. We sent in the president of our locality's committee, but she just pointed at her stupid letter. Says dogs have rights too. Can you believe it?'

'I mean,' ventured Natasha, 'I do believe in animal welfare.'

'Of course,' said Mrs Khanna. 'But we humans have some rights too in the houses we buy and maintain, do we not? I can't even entertain at home for all the ruckus that woman's infernal animals make. We can't walk in the street for fear they'll charge. It's not sustainable.'

'No.' Natasha thought of Navya, who had no fear. She'd reach out and pet any animal that came near her, and Natasha was forever telling her to take care, to find out from an owner first if the animal was friendly before approaching it. And they lived right opposite that feral pack. 'No,' she said.

'I mean, she's turned the street into a zoo. We have tried everything as a community. No one talks to Sunny, no one is friends with her teenage daughter, but they don't care. They come in, they go out, bold as you please.' Mrs Khanna sniffed with righteous anger. 'Anytime we send animal rescue to the house, she waves that damned letter at the officers and threatens them with ministerial action. When all our entreaties failed, we even cancelled her refuse collection, but she just flung her rubbish out onto the street.' Mrs Khanna shook her head with sadness. 'The woman's impossible.'

It had been a busy day, with clients cancelling tickets all the way to the end of the year. She had tried to offer them vouchers for future travel, but they had all opted for refunds instead, and as she had reported on her day's activities to her boss, he had told her he was unsure how much longer he could continue to keep the agency going. 'I know the PM says we can't fire people,' he had said, 'but I don't even know if I can continue to pay myself.'

Natasha had told him she understood, but when she had tried to speak to Jussie, he had been busy. 'I've got to finish this report,' he had said to her, 'I'll come and find you once it is done.'

He had skipped lunch, remaining holed up in his study as the day turned to night. He had only emerged, exhausted and ravenous, after Navya was in bed, and had launched straight into the problems he was facing with a junior analyst. 'She's so slow, Tasha,' he was saying as he stuffed an entire roti into his mouth. 'And when I finally do get her work, I have to spend the entire day fixing her mistakes.'

This was her cue to sympathise, but Natasha found herself frowning. 'I'm not happy here.'

Jussie looked up. Natasha paused. That wasn't what she had meant to say at all, but now that she had his attention, the words spilled out. She didn't talk about her job or his absence from their lives, but about how unhappy she was in the flat. Shivani spoke about negative energy; perhaps it was the neighbourhood's unfriendliness that was causing their woes.

Jussie looked stunned. 'But we've just moved here.'

'Things don't feel right. No one is friendly; no one makes an effort.'

'People are busy.'

'With what?'

'Come on, Natasha, be reasonable. Give it some time.'

'I don't have a single friend here, Jussie. And you're always busy with your work. I sometimes go days without talking to a single adult.'

Jussie made a soothing sound. A few of his friends were in fear of being fired, and others had spoken of taking pay cuts. Just the other day, he had told her about a restaurateur friend who was having to close a new restaurant before it even opened to the public. He ran a hand through his hair, and she wondered if his hairline was starting to recede. 'This time is tricky for all of us, darling.'

'I know, Jussie,' Natasha said, already feeling bad for burdening him with her small troubles. She put an arm on his shoulder. 'And I'm sorry. Things *will* improve.'

The dogs barked late into the night. One took up a howl, a long, slow, uninterrupted note of longing or of despair, and the others joined its refrain. Soon barks were added to the mix, and as Natasha sat up in bed, she saw that it was nearly three in the morning. She lay back down and buried her head under her pillow.

At four, Jussie rose. He sat up in bed for a while, his eyes still clouded with sleep, and Natasha watched him silently. He muttered about the noise, pummelled his pillows and tried to return to sleep without success. The dogs continued to bark, and at length, he rose and disappeared into his study. Navya slept undisturbed, thank heavens, but Natasha knew how little sleep her husband was functioning on.

At five in the morning, the dogs were still barking loudly. Natasha got up, wrapped a dressing gown around herself and walked out. She had only been out of the house a handful of times since lockdown had begun, but now she opened her gate, taking in the dewy morning air and the relentless barking of the dogs. Jussie's study lay towards the back of the flat, but it would be a miracle if he was able to concentrate on his work. She inhaled deeply, and the motion appeared to give her resolve, for she crossed the street and rang Sunny's bell. The dogs paused at her noise and then took up where they had left off, louder, if that were possible.

No movement could be heard from inside the house, and after waiting for a minute or so, Natasha rang the bell again. Only this time, she pushed down on the buzzer and maintained her pressure until the owner of the dogs made her appearance.

She appeared disturbed by the bell, running her hands through dishevelled hair, and then blinking as she recognised her visitor. 'What,' she asked irritably, 'is the meaning of this?'

'It was a bit loud, wasn't it?'

'A bit loud?' answered Sunny, incredulous. 'A *bit* loud? It's five in the morning, for God's sake.'

'I apologise for my noise,' said Natasha in a sympathetic tone. 'I timed myself and it seems I rang your bell continuously for five minutes.'

Sunny bristled with irritation. 'The noise was unbearable.'

'I can imagine,' said Natasha. 'So, you can understand how unbearable your dogs' barking all night has been for the neighbourhood.'

Mrs Bose watched the exchange from her balcony. 'You tell her,' she called out, pumping her fist in the air. 'I've been unable to sleep on many nights on account of her mongrels.'

'I thought you were nice,' Sunny spat out, 'but you're just like the rest of this nosy, interfering community. Do you know, they refused to pick up my rubbish?'

'I'm not saying they are the most welcoming people,' replied Natasha calmly, 'but as far as I can see it, you're part of the problem.'

Sunny laughed in disbelief.

'I haven't been able to sleep all night. Neither has my husband. Neither,' she added, pointing towards Mrs Bose on her balcony, 'has the rest of this lousy neighbourhood. And I agree that my pressing down on a buzzer for five minutes was unreasonable. But so is your keeping thirty dogs you can't keep quiet at night.'

The dogs were still barking, and Sunny gritted her teeth. She stared at Natasha, as if seeing her for the first time. She looked the woman up and down, taking in her baby pink satin dressing gown and chappals painted the colour of the Brazilian flag, and laughed. 'I don't have to listen to you,' she said as she shut her gate.

Natasha rang the doorbell again, keeping her finger pressed until the scowling woman opened the door once more. 'I can keep this up for as long as your dogs can,' she replied. 'And I may look meek and compliant, but I am determined and I am organised. I can make sure there is someone at your door all the time.' Natasha paused, hoping Sunny didn't see through her bluff. 'I can have someone here day and night, filling your ears with noise until you decide to stop doing the same to us.' She looked firmly at Sunny, refusing to smile, refusing to look away even as her adversary watched her wordlessly.

Natasha lifted her finger from the buzzer, continuing to stare at the other woman. She saw the woman blink, saw her sigh as the unpleasant clang of the doorbell abated, and she turned around and walked back towards her home. As she opened her gate, Mrs Bose got onto her feet on her balcony and applauded. 'Well done, *Beta*,' she said to

Natasha. 'Hopefully you've managed to talk some sense into that woman.'

The dogs didn't bark that night. There was the occasional flare-up, but nothing on the scale of the previous night. Natasha enjoyed going to bed in a home that grew silent just as the city had, and Jussie slept so soundly that it was Navya who woke him up in the morning.

'Come, Papa,' she urged. 'I want to show you where Mama and I leave the bread out for the birds. Or,' and here she lowered her voice to a whisper, cupping her hands to her father's ear, 'for when the leopards come to Delhi.'

There was an excuse on Jussie's lips, but he looked at his daughter, so wide-eyed, so hopeful, and nodded. They went outside together. Natasha knew Navya wanted to impress her father. She knew that she wanted to show him a leopard so he would spend his morning with her, or to show him a domesticated cat if a wild one proved elusive, and she watched as her daughter held on to her father's hand tightly, as if she was scared he would disappear if she let go.

'Mama bought me a 200-piece puzzle,' Navya said, showing off. 'Would you like to do it with me?'

Jussie smiled. 'A 200-piece puzzle, huh?' He looked at his watch. The sun was beating down on them, and as Natasha looked at the lawn, she saw the glass panel of the mailbox glint in the light. Mr Rastogi had deposited the latest offering for Navya's book club. In a while she would go and retrieve the book and put it on the table to disinfect. In a while she would think of breakfast and of Jussie's morning coffee. For the moment, though, she sat down on her table and chair set and watched as father and daughter laid out fresh breadcrumbs for any birds or cats or leopards that chose to pay them a visit.

The Journey Home

And still they walked, the others in their thousands.

Shyam, the delivery boy who occupied the room next to Chhote Lal's, left almost as soon as lockdown began. His family was in Bihar, same as Chhote Lal's, and he planned to make his way back home after work slowed down. He had been uncertain of how he would travel. Public transport had been stopped almost as soon as they had heard of the lockdown, and he had no private mode of travel. He had been in the habit of sending the bulk of his salary to his family in the village, and as the company that employed him dispensed with his services, Shyam had almost immediately run out of money.

He had begun to walk then, in early April, charting out his route on his smart phone. Chhote Lal had pointed out that it was a distance of thousands of kilometres, that he would be walking on hot tar in beat-up shoes, and that his phone would run out of battery before the first day was up, but the boy had pointed heavenwards, and Chhote Lal knew that Shyam had no other options. He knew that offices and factories were shutting down across the country, and that employers were laying off blue collar workers without ceremony. Shyam didn't ask him for a loan, and though Chhote Lal had little to spare, he gave him a thousand rupees. He hadn't heard from him since he left, and when Chhote Lal had tried to call him, his number had been unreachable. It was now weeks after his departure, and there had been no news of the boy. No one else had heard from him either and Chote Lal prayed that he had reached home, safe and disease-free.

Normally, the stretch of the year between February and May was Chhote Lal's busiest time. It was when everyone had their homes painted for the year. He'd been busy in February, busy in the first week of March, when he had sent his savings over to his family in Bihar, but as the days advanced to the middle of the month, he found people cancelling their bookings.

'It's not safe,' he heard again and again. 'Just stay in your home, stay safe, and we'll call you over once the threat of this virus has passed.'

'Don't worry,' he told them as they apologised. 'I have enough for now, and it's just a matter of a few weeks, in any case. I'll be painting your home before the monsoon arrives.' Mr Choudhury, who he had been due to work for next, offered to pay him the fee that had been promised, but Chhote Lal refused. 'Pay me,' he told the man, 'when I have done the work.'

The threat didn't pass, bedding down in Mumbai and radiating out to the rest of the country, and no one called him to come over and paint their homes.

His family in Bihar remained safe, thank heavens. They had sufficient funds for their needs, but as lockdown was extended, once and then again, Chhote Lal began to wonder how long it would be before the money he had sent them ran out. He wanted to return to his work. His cash reserves were running down, and after mulling matters over in his head, he thought to contact Mr Rastogi and Mr Choudhury, two next-door neighbours who had always been kind to him. He had been safe in his room, avoiding outside contact, and he would walk to the neighbourhood, not meeting anyone. He would wear the Madhubani mask his wife had stitched and sent for him, and surely, with these precautions, it would be safe for him to work.

But when he called Mr Rastogi, the old man laughed. 'Arre, Chhote Lal, my daughter will kill me if she even hears about anyone looking at the house. She has spies everywhere, you know. To be honest, she terrifies me more than this virus does.'

'Yes, sir,' Chhote Lal replied, telling himself there was no point talking to Mr Choudhury. They were all hunkering down, all of India, all of the world, and he would not be allowed in for all the precautions he took.

His family in the village didn't ask him for money, but he knew things were far from comfortable. Ordinarily, he sent money home on the first of every month, but this year, three months had passed without any remittances having been made. In Delhi too, his supplies were running low. He had enough rice and daal to last him a week, maybe more if he economised, but he had stopped purchasing fresh vegetables from the market.

Then one weekend, his wife called to tell him their youngest child had a cold.

'It's not the virus, is it?'

'No,' she said haltingly. 'I don't think it is. Where would he have met someone with the virus?'

'What are you giving him?'

'Turmeric milk,' she said. 'I hope that is sufficient.'

'Have you consulted the doctor?'

'No,' she said. She didn't justify her decision, but she didn't have to. She hadn't seen any money from him for all of the year's house painting season.

Chhote Lal called Mr Choudhury the next day. 'Sir,' he said after they had both asked after the other's wellbeing. 'Sir, I want you to know I've been taking every possible precaution.'

'It's no less than I'd expect of you,' replied Mr Choudhury. 'You've always been level-headed.'

'I've made sure to avoid all contact with the outside world.'

'Very good.'

'Sir,' Chote Lal continued in a hesitant voice, 'don't you think it would be ok for me to come and paint the house now?'

There was a long pause before the man at the other end sighed. 'Chhote Lal,' said Mr Choudhury. 'You know it's not safe right now.'

'Yes, sir,' replied Chhote Lal. 'Of course, sir.'

He was on the point of saying goodbye when Mr Choudhury asked, 'Do you need for anything?'

'Sir?' Chhote Lal said, sniffing in his embarrassment.

'Do you need money? I know you aren't able to work at the moment.'

'Sir,' said Chhote Lal, clenching and unclenching his fists. He wasn't in the habit of quoting for his work. His business was built on word of mouth, with a satisfied customer telling friends what they paid for his services, and he had been able to carry on working for years without once referring to money. He sat down on his bed and considered his words carefully. 'Sir, my son is ill in the village. And no one wants their walls painted at the moment.'

'Oh,' asked Mr Choudhury, 'is it serious?'

'My wife hopes it isn't.'

'Has he seen the doctor?'

'No, sir.'

'He has to see the doctor, Chhote Lal.'

'Yes, sir.'

There was another long pause. Mr Choudhury waited for Chhote Lal to tell him that an appointment had been booked, perhaps. 'Look,' he finally said. 'We both know that as long as this virus doesn't kill us, you will return here to paint my house. It may be in one month, it may be in six, but you will return. So why don't I give you an advance—not free money, mind you—just half the money you have coming to you once you can return to work.'

'No, no,' said Chhote Lal. He stood up in his agitation, even though Mr Choudhury couldn't see him. 'Please,' he said. 'I didn't call to ask for money, only to ask for work.'

'I know,' replied Mr Choudhury. 'And I do want you to work for me, but only when it is safe. Let me pay you an advance in the meantime so your son can be seen by a doctor.'

Mr Choudhury wouldn't listen to his protests, and by the end of the conversation, the matter was settled. Chhote Lal walked to the gates of the neighbourhood, where Mr Choudhury waited. He held an envelope out, telling Chhote Lal not to open it for three days for fear of contagion. Chhote Lal followed his instructions, and when he did open the envelope, he found Mr Choudhury had paid more than half his fee for painting.

When he called to protest, Mr Choudhury said, 'I'm factoring in inflation. This is exactly half of what I mean to pay you. Don't go expecting any more.' Chhote Lal stuttered his thanks, and Mr Choudhury replied, 'Make sure your boy consults the doctor.'

A week later, Mr Rastogi called him. 'I hear this scoundrel Choudhury is trying to book you, but don't forget you committed to me first.'

'Sir …'

'Come to the neighbourhood gates this evening then, and I'll get Chetan to hand over an advance.'

'But, sir …'

'No but-vut,' the old man said. 'I don't want that Choudhury sneaking in and monopolising you. Remember, this evening at the gates. 6 p.m. sharp.'

Chhote Lal's son's illness turned out to be a summer time sniffle, as unremarkable as it was unexpected, and it vanished before the call could be placed to the doctor. There was no news, in the meantime, of Shyam. When he went out to his little market at the end of his street to fetch supplies, Chhote Lal would sometimes hear news of migrant workers making their way back home.

Dayal, the shopkeeper, kept his TV permanently tuned to the news. 'They're still walking, the poor sods.'

'If only they could have stayed here.'

'How could they?' Dayal replied. 'God knows I miss their custom, but for weeks I had been giving them their food on credit.'

'I lent my neighbour a little too,' Chhote Lal said. 'He told me he would be sure to repay it. He said that he would contact me as soon as he reached his village …'

'Heaven only knows if they will ever reach home. There's talk of not letting them into the villages now for fear of the virus.'

'It's a miserable situation.'

An image of a woman carrying a toddler on the motorway flickered on the screen. The child was around the same age as Chhote Lal's son, and naked apart from a faded pair of shorts. Its hair was matted, its cheeks red from the sun, and it dug its face into its mother's shoulders for some respite from the heat. The woman, a slight creature, adjusted her child's head to allow her to see the road ahead, and continued to walk slowly. She dragged her feet, and Chhote Lal knew her slippers had all but collapsed. Dayal turned to switch the TV off. He touched his fingertips to his forehead and bowed before the image of the Goddess Lakshmi near his till. 'I'm alive,' he said. 'You're alive. It feels ungrateful to ask for any more at a time like this.'

It was mid-June when private buses began running to transport migrant workers home. The ticket price was steeper than expected, but Chhote Lal had money left over from the advance he had been paid. He worried, though, about when he would be able to return, and he called Mr Choudhury to offer to work for him before he left.

'Do you need money for the ticket, Chhote Lal?'

'No, sir,' replied the man. 'I have enough, thanks to your and Rastogi sir's generosity. But I didn't want to leave without finishing the work.'

'You'll return,' said Mr Choudhury. 'But in the meantime, come take some more money.' Chhote Lal protested, but Mr Choudhury told him he wouldn't want to return to his family empty-handed. 'You'll want to buy sweets for your children. You'll want to make sure everyone is comfortable at home. Just take something small at this stage, and we will keep accounts for when you're back.'

He travelled then, but as June turned to July, as the monsoons ravaged the country, as August came to an end, he called Mr Choudhury. 'I feel very bad about having taken your money without painting your house, Sir.'

'Chote Lal,' said Mr Choudhury, 'You're planning on returning to Delhi, aren't you?'

'Yes, sir.'

'Then the painting can wait.'

There was no mention of the money that had been pressed on him. 'But,' said Chote Lal, 'the house must be looking dirty. It should have been fresh and clean by now.' Mr Choudhury laughed. 'The rain has taken care of that,' he said, 'and besides, it's not like we have a parade of visitors this year.' He paused, and Chote Lal could hear him lifting a cup to his mouth. He took a deep draught and sighed his pleasure. 'But tell me this,' he said, 'you and your family are all well, aren't you?'

'Yes, sir,' Chhote Lal said. 'It feels good to be able to keep my family safe. And my wife has started to make masks with her Madhubani fabric, which have been selling well in Mumbai. But I owe you and Rastogi sir money, and I just don't feel easy without having paid you back.'

'Don't worry about that,' Mr Choudhury said gruffly, and then, 'Does your wife have a website?'

'She sells on WhatsApp.'

Designs were sent across to Mr Choudhury's phone, and Mr Choudhury messaged him to tell him his wife and daughter had fallen in love with the masks. 'They're so much smarter than the utilitarian masks you see on the internet. Can I place an order for a few?'

Chhote Lal said the postal service was still temperamental, and that he would be in touch when it was running reliably, but the next day, he dusted off his old creaking cycle, applying oil on the joints until it moved smoothly, and travelled to the next village, where a postal service operated. He posted half a dozen face masks for the Choudhury family, and then, another few for Mr Rastogi and his daughter. They wouldn't let him return to work, but they wouldn't be able to prevent him from repaying their care with his own.

Balcony Notes

Her timing, Mahima realised, couldn't have been worse. It was a big enough upheaval to move across continents, it was a big enough undertaking to move in with your mother-in-law, and it was a sheer test of forbearance to do all this a week before lockdown began.

Her promised job disappeared before the month was out. They hadn't completed the joining formalities before the move, and as she hadn't heard from the paper, she had called her line manager, Amrita, to ask if she were to commence work on the first of the month.

She knew there was no going out just then, and she added with a nervous, new joiner's laugh, that she realised it would be the 1st of April—'You know, April Fool's Day'—and Amrita asked her if HR had been in touch.

'No.'

'They should have been. And I should have thought of calling you too.'

Mahima was on the verge of saying that the silence was understandable given the circumstances, but she wasn't sure what Amrita's words presaged, and remained quiet.

'It's been crazy round here, anyway,' Amrita was saying, talking too fast, her words blurring into one another, and Mahima knew bad news was coming. 'Our ad revenues have fallen off a cliff, and people have been cancelling newspaper orders across the country.' She sighed. 'They're not even letting the paper delivery boys inside neighbourhoods now for fear of the virus.'

There was a long pause after which Mahima said, 'It's a strange time.'

'It is,' Amrita agreed. 'It is all counterintuitive, but we've seen this thing spread across the world, and now we're scared of our own shadows. My mother-in-law,' and here came a conspiratorial laugh, 'won't even let us buy chicken for fear of the virus.'

'Mothers-in-law ...'

'It's stupid,' she said, 'but there is all this information proliferating on the internet. On social media, on WhatsApp groups blaming China, blaming sections of society …'

'My mother-in-law is the same,' said Mahima. She wished Amrita would get to the point. 'Blaming India's coronavirus spread on the Jamatis. As if Hindus and Sikhs haven't been congregating all this while.' She paused as she heard silence at the other end. 'As if violence wasn't unleashed on the streets of Delhi during Trump's visit this time last month.'

'I know,' said Amrita, sighing again. 'It's all a nightmare, and we can't report it if they won't buy our papers. My advice to you is to contact one of these online papers. *The Wire*, *Scroll*, etc, etc. They're well run and not in danger of losing readers.'

Mahima winced. 'But …'

'I'm sorry, Mahima,' the woman said. 'I'll make sure HR is in touch.'

Mahima sat unemployed for months. Applications were sent to all the news sites she came across, in India and abroad, but all she had to show on her CV was a couple of years at an accountancy firm followed by a master's in creative writing. They were all chasing the same dozen jobs, all of India's experienced and newly redundant journalists, and all the others from the rest of the world too, and she told herself it wasn't a surprise that her applications weren't so much as warranting a response.

Rahul's job, luckily, was unaffected. He'd transferred from his law firm in London to its India office, and though the idea was to move to Mumbai to join the bigger team there, for the moment, virtual working sufficed. For the moment, the room they shared in Rahul's mother's flat in Delhi sufficed, and for the moment, Mahima didn't complain.

She didn't tell him how unmoored she felt through the day. She didn't tell him how the sounds of his mother praying on the balcony woke her up every day, didn't tell him her heart sank as he disappeared off to work after breakfast while his mother busied herself with her chores, didn't tell him she offered to help with lunch or dinner but was always rebuffed. His mother had her routines; prayers and meals at fixed hours, the sleepy hours of the afternoon spent catching up with friends or her sisters, and Mahima always felt she was in the way.

She worked hard to make herself as unobtrusive as possible. She didn't tell Rahul that for fear of looking work-shy in his mother's house, she didn't read, didn't listen to music, didn't even put on the TV. She didn't tell him she didn't talk on the phone to her friends in London for fear of her mother-in-law thinking her idle and limited herself to contacting her parents through text in case she sounded hostile to the woman of the house.

She didn't tell him how lonely she felt in this city, even though she had grown up here, and even though she was only a few miles away from her parents' home. For all that Rahul's Delhi was familiar to her—there was a press-wallah here as well as in her parents' neighbourhood; there was a child downstairs she could hear here just as she could in her parents' neighbourhood; there was the smell of incense in the living room just as there was in her parents' home; there was the Ramayana playing just as there was in her parents' home, there was the same beloved, lilting, half-spoken, half-sung Hindi words on people's lips, but it was all there and never quite the same for her, the neighbours, the conversations, the belonging, familiar as it had been when she had been a chlid, but forever out of reach in his mother's house.

Rahul understood, though. He didn't say anything to her directly, but when they were both in bed, he would speak to her of restarting their search for their Mumbai home. He knew, as she did, that the prospect of travel and of entering strangers' homes was a distant one, but he sensed that planning a future together gave her something to look forward to.

'We'll have a place by the sea,' he would start, whispering for fear of his mother overhearing.

'And a large balcony?'

'Come here,' Rahul would tell his wife, and they would both pull the bedspread over themselves as if that offered extra insulation against eavesdroppers. 'A large balcony overlooking the sea.'

'We'll fill it with plants.'

'It'll be our very own garden by the sea.'

Mahima laughed at the thought, and his hand was instantly cupped over her mouth, muffling her noise. 'The parties we'll have …'

'Mojitos by the beach.'

'Mmm,' she sighed, settling herself against the crook of his arm. 'Mojitos by the beach.'

Ma liked sitting on the balcony after breakfast. She would turn on the fan that hung from the ceiling and sit quietly looking out onto the street. A few weeks into her stay, Mahima began to join her. She had hesitated to intrude, and had not wanted to look idle, but as the days passed, she worried she was looking unfriendly, and one morning, as the older woman stepped out to the balcony, Mahima brought her a cup of tea. Ma looked surprised at her daughter-in-law's presence, but not averse to the company, and the routine had been established.

Ma complained about how quiet it was in those early weeks. She told Mahima that in the pre-lockdown days, after the children had been dispatched to their schools and the men had gone to their offices, the women of the neighbourhood gathered for their morning walks. They would behave like ruffians, Ma told her laughing, like small-town gangsters, walking in the middle of the road and holding up traffic, trading loud jokes, shelling peanuts and discarding the shells on the streets. 'It's the older ones who were always the worst,' Ma said. 'They've paid their dues to society. They've brought up their children and married them off, and now they think they don't owe anything to anyone.'

'Were you one of the morning walk gangsters, Ma?'

'Me?' smiled Ma. 'No. What do I have to do with such frivolity?' Still, she smiled at the thought, and as the press-wallah passed by, bringing the house next door their ironing, she smiled at his salute: 'Ram-Ram, Mrs. Bose!' Ma began to point out the faces that sometimes appeared. 'There's no life, no movement right now,' she told Mahima, 'But if you look carefully, you'll notice things.'

'Do you sit out every day?' The temperature was nearing 40, and, Mahima realised, it had been a decade or longer since she had experienced a Delhi summer.

'Every day,' said Ma proudly. 'And I know everything that goes on around here.' She pointed across the street and said, 'Can you see that boy in the garden?'

Mahima nodded, as a teenager in a bright red tee-shirt and a baseball cap walked in a garden, his arms swinging as he moved. He appeared distracted for someone who seemed to be out for the purpose of exercise; his pace was too slow, but he didn't appear to have any other goal. He was alone, wasn't reading, wasn't on the phone either, and Mahima looked at her mother-in-law in inquiry.

'He's in love with the girl in the next house,' Ma explained. 'She's the daughter of the dog woman. He's probably hoping to catch sight of her.'

'They're not together?'

'How would I know?' replied Ma nonchalantly. 'It's not like it's a matter that is of any interest to me.'

The child downstairs, a little girl called Navya, ventured out one morning in the early days of lockdown. She was alone, unattended by her mother, who was a smiling, nervous little thing. The girl quietly took out a rickety wooden ladder and perched it precariously on the uneven ground between lawn and concrete slabbing. 'Look,' whispered Ma, holding a finger to her lips, and Mahima looked to where she indicated.

The girl began to climb the ladder, and Mahima was up on her feet. 'But it isn't safe,' and Ma pulled her down.

'Wait,' she said. 'The girl is on a mission.'

And sure enough, Navya was talking to Mr Rastogi next door, who was urging her off the ladder. The women watched as he came round to the gate, a book in his hand, and stood talking to the child. 'What's in this tea?' asked Ma suddenly.

'Cardamom,' replied Mahima, 'and a little ground pepper. There's a restaurant in London that serves its tea this way.' She looked at her mother-in-law and laughed. 'We took you there when you visited, remember. How expensive you said everything was.'

'Yes, yes,' exclaimed Ma. 'Imagine charging a thousand rupees for three pieces of papdi!' She shuddered, then took another sip. 'Still,' she said, as she watched the old man talk to the child. 'It does taste nice.'

Nothing was mentioned for a while. Mahima was uncertain whether Rahul had told his mother about her job offer being withdrawn, but it was clear that while he disappeared to their bedroom to work every morning, his wife lingered, helping Ma prepare breakfast and lunch, spending time on the balcony, and engaging in no pursuit more productive than the reading of the news.

To her credit, Ma never said anything directly, but over time, the hints grew broader. Ma began to bring out chores with her to the balcony, telling Mahima she couldn't bear to sit idle. She would bring out huge rounds of watermelon, and though Mahima volunteered herself for the task, Ma would sit herself down on the floor as her daughter-in-law protested, plunging her knife into the flesh of the fruit, tearing it into bright, bleeding strips. 'You sit,' she would say sweetly, as she massaged her shoulder with the effort of her task. 'You enjoy your tea.'

Mahima complained to Rahul that his mother was showing her up on purpose, but Rahul shook his head. 'Think about it,' he told her. 'She's been living alone all these years. She is used to keeping herself busy.'

Mahima didn't ask him if he had spoken to his mother about her lack of employment, scared of seeming paranoid. Ma *had* welcomed her in, enveloping her into her routine, not complaining when she had slept in on account of her jetlag, not complaining either that Mahima's food was too mild for her tastes even as her son ladled slivers of green chilli onto anything Mahima prepared. She had never been known for small talk, but if she had been inconvenienced by Mahima's presence, she never let on. And still it irked Mahima, her mother-in-law's sudden industriousness.

As it grew hotter, Delhi began to look like a facsimile of its former self. You heard children's voices now. They rode their bikes, they stood outside their friends' doors. They didn't congregate; there was still too much to fear, and the morning walk gangsters no longer terrorised the streets, but traffic was starting to pick up. The ice cream man plied his trade around the neighbourhood's streets once more; the press-wallah passed by more often, his hand raised in a salute at the sight of Ma. There was more to see, more than just the boy opposite looking out for the girl he loved, and now that Ma had acquainted Mahima with all the street's characters and their dramas she found herself looking forward to observing their days.

One morning, Ma asked Mahima if she regretted her degree.

'My degree?'

'Yes,' she said. 'Not your bachelors, but the creative writing one.' Mahima didn't speak, and Ma added, 'I wonder if you would have been happier staying in accounting.'

'I would probably still be employed, for one,' Mahima said with a little laugh.

Ma didn't respond immediately, and instead she fanned her face with a hand. 'Routine,' she said, when she spoke, 'is always helpful, of course, and community too. Being part of a team, having a reason to change out of your pyjamas in the morning … but it's more than that, it's the feeling that you are useful. I mean,' and here she looked at her hands, 'I've so enjoyed having you children with me. I've loved hacking into whole watermelons for the both of you even though you think me silly.'

'I don't think you're silly, Ma,' Mahima said. 'I would love to be as busy as you are.'

'That's what I want for you too, Beta,' said Ma. 'Not the hacking into watermelons, which *is* silly, but it keeps an old woman occupied. I want for you to be using your brain like Rahul gets to. I want for you to feel fulfilled.'

Mahima was quiet. She thought of the many job applications she had sent out. She hadn't had a single response, and now that she thought about it, she hadn't sent a follow-up in weeks. She had just sort of given up as bad news spread across the world. Travel magazines were retrenching or shutting down, as were print publications. Mahima had thought several times of reaching out to Amrita, her old would-be line manager, but she knew she would be fighting for her job too.

Ma was watching her, and she looked out onto the street. Out by the gate, Navya and Mr Rastogi were carrying out a conversation. 'Mahima,' Ma was saying to her, 'I can't pretend to know how tough this is for you. But I've gotten to know you over the past few months, and I know you're kind and observant, and I know you want to write. What I don't know is why you don't.'

Later that evening, Rahul spoke about Mumbai. 'You must be restless, stuck out here with only Ma for company.'

'It's not so bad.'

He reached his hand out to hers. They still lay under a bed spread, still spoke in whispers for fear of disturbing his mother. 'They're talking about returning to the office from next month,' he said.

'You said that last month.'

'Yes,' he said, 'but I'm thinking, if this does go ahead, this return to the office, maybe we should go to Mumbai for a couple of days beforehand to have a look at some properties.' He was looking at her under the diffused light of the bedspread, waiting for her reaction, and she nodded. She didn't tell him about the worries she had, of the taxi journey to the airport or of the air circulating on the plane, of the cleanliness of the homes they would visit or the germs they could transmit to his mother on their return.

'I mean, it may not go ahead. Lockdown could be extended, but I thought you'd like to plan for our move,' he said, as he reached across her to turn off the light.

Inspiration refused to strike. For days she sat out with Ma after breakfast, watching as the street grew in traffic. The dogs, used for so long to lording over the unoccupied road, barked anytime traffic passed, and passers-by had taken to walking with sticks or long umbrellas to protect themselves. Friends still didn't hang out together, spending time instead outside each other's gates.

The little girl, Navya, who had formed a firm friendship with the old man next door, seemed to have grown taller. One day, she looked up at the balcony and Mahima waved. Navya waved back, a book in her hand. She walked out of the house, depositing the book in Mr Rastogi's letter box, before returning to her garden, where her mother waited.

Mahima waved at her. 'What a strange time this is.'

The woman gave a nod. 'Yes,' she said, 'it's a once in a century event, they say.'

They exchanged some desultory words when Mahima remembered the note she hadn't answered. 'I owe you an apology.'

'No, no,' said the woman, her hands jangling with her bangles. She looked up, shading her eyes, and though she smiled, Mahima could see she waited for an explanation.

'I do owe you an apology,' she said. 'I got your message, but lockdown had begun and I didn't want to send a message back down for fear of putting any of my germs on a piece of paper.'

The woman—Mahima thought she was called Natasha—laughed. 'What an odd time the very beginning of lockdown was.'

'It was,' Mahima said with a smile. 'And after all this is done, I'd love to take you up on that drink.'

'What drink?' asked Navya.

'Well …'

'And,' Mahima broke in, 'I would love to trouble you,' pointing at Navya, 'for your recommendation on what to read.' The mother laughed, and Mahima nodded, 'I see she has a nice little library system going with Mr Rastogi.'

'Not a library. It's a book club,' said the child. 'We call it the New New-Delhi Book Club.'

'The New New-Delhi Book Club?'

'Because,' said the child, all seriousness, 'the city is called New Delhi. And our book club is new. That is why we call it The New New-Delhi Book Club.'

'That is a very good name.'

'It is,' said the girl proudly. 'And we read some very good books.'

'Can you recommend something to me?'

'Well,' said the child, pondering the question as her mother threw back her head and laughed. A tiny diamond glinted in her nose. 'Mr Rastogi has just given me his daughter's copy of *Harry Potter and the Philosopher's Stone*.'

'And you're reading it?'

'Yes,' she said, nodding. She screwed her mouth together till it resembled a rosebud, and confided, 'My mum is helping me a little bit. It *is* a little scary, but as long as you're not made to sleep in a cupboard, I think you'll enjoy it.'

'Navya!' exclaimed her scandalised mother.

Ma also appeared in the balcony. 'I would never let her sleep in a cupboard,' she told the child. 'A smelly boy, perhaps, but never her.'

Later that day, Mahima went out onto the balcony. For all the animation that was slowly returning to Delhi, at that hour, the city was utterly still. Maybe everyone was taking their afternoon nap. The dogs from across the street lay sleeping on the pavement. There was no dawdling passer-by, no worker on an errand, no sound of a screaming child or of a domestic row. Everything was quiet. Mahima went in and brought out her notebook and pen. She wrote a sentence:

Her timing, she realised, couldn't have been worse.

She read the words and nodded. From across the road, the lovelorn boy gazed at his neighbour's lawn. Mahima turned back to her page, rereading her solitary line. This wasn't a job. This wasn't a future. It wasn't anything more than the hint of a beginning, the hope of one word following another, but it was something. She smiled as the boy slowly disappeared indoors. This was something.

Justice of A Sort

So pleasant she had seemed at the start, that woman with her large-large eyes and her ready smiles. She had come in wearing a floating pink salwar kameez, a silver toe ring glinting on her toe, as if she was on holiday by a beach somewhere. She was a smiling, wafting advert for a tropical getaway—her skin glowing, her hair long and lustrous—but I was sure the closest this upstart got to an island paradise was when she applied foul-smelling, waxy coconut oil into her hair every morning.

'I'm Natasha,' she had said in a rushed, breathy voice. She had come in with a fruit basket, as an introduction, as if the delivery vans that had obstructed half the street for an entire day hadn't been calling card enough. She had looked down and around my front yard, and I had known immediately that she would be trouble. Her smile dimmed as she saw the dogs. They had barely raised their heads at her approach, and let's face it, she was the one encroaching on their territory anyway, but her voice rose, her imbecilic breathiness died away, and she said in clipped, precise tones, 'How many do you have?'

I sighed. 'At the moment,' I told her, 'I have twenty-eight.'

She winced at my words. *She* winced, as if the inconvenience was hers. As if it was her having to rescue and care for the poor things as they lay abandoned and unwanted on street corners. As they were chased by all—by the area's security guards, by the neighbourhood's hooligan children, by the police, by the rash motorists, by even the animal 'welfare' officers who looked to euthanise them.

There was no one else in the area to look out for them, and even that one heartbreaking time a litter of puppies had been found next to their dead mother, in the dip in the road next to the temple, no one's heart had melted. They all professed their sorrow, sure. They all plastered the poor animals' cute pictures on Facebook, musing about the cruel arbitrariness of life, but not a single person offered their help. I was the only one to suggest the puppies be given a home. I was the only one who watched as they all, one after the other, said that they couldn't help out. They were too busy, their homes were too crowded, their children and in-laws too time consuming, they said, even as they bent over the poor puppies to take a better photo.

I'd been the one who had taken them in. They'd applauded me then. They'd said I had a large heart, when really, my greatest utility had been in ridding the area of those little critters while sparing their conscience. 'You're a lion,' they'd said. 'A true hero.' And yet, when the poor, distraught, transplanted souls had cried in the night for the loss of mother and home, they'd begun to make objections. 'Can't you keep them quiet?' they'd asked, and the chief of the complainers, that nosy, opinionated Mrs Bose, had approached me with a suggestion.

'What is that thing they give to babies to keep them quiet?'

I'd been up all night, tending to the new arrivals, the smallest of whom would only drink milk from a bottle held by me, and I blinked uncomprehendingly at her.

'You know,' she said, impatient, already irritated by the dogs at my doorstep. 'Those dummy things.'

'Dummy?'

'Uff, those … what do you call them,' she said crossly, 'those pacifier things. Can't you just stuff one of those things in their mouths?'

Buddy, my Alsatian, opened his mouth in a yawn, and I bent to stroke him behind the ear. Mrs Bose was standing in front of me expectantly, hand on hip, and I pointed to the dog's open mouth. 'You expect a dummy to work on him?'

'Well,' she blustered. 'He's a fully grown dog. Surely there must be something that would work.'

'They've just lost their mother,' I said. 'And you expect them not to grieve?'

'A muzzle,' Mrs Bose countered triumphantly. 'You could muzzle them!'

My head was throbbing with lack of sleep, and I stared hard at her. My vision blurred. It was growing hot, the sun piercing, and I felt myself sway. Mrs Bose continued to stare at me as I spoke, 'It's like if I asked you to put masking tape on your mouth. Would that be acceptable, Mrs Bose?'

The heat rose. Mrs Bose blinked at me. 'Tell me, would you think it was reasonable if I asked you to wear a muzzle in your own home?'

They had set up a friendship, the newcomer Natasha and Mrs Bose's daughter-in-law. I'd seen them talk at the gate to their house before we entered lockdown, and a couple of times, I'd seen the women point their heads towards my door. Laughter would follow, which would set the dogs off, and the two mean-spirited women would shake their pretty heads in disapproval.

Rajan and the children told me to disregard them, but it was hard not to feel hemmed in by all the ill-will from our neighbours. We didn't have a single local friend in the area, and no one checked in on us as we entered lockdown. They were all at it, gossiping across their fences about all the supplies they had stocked up on. They laughed about their children worrying about Maggi noodles more than about rice or lentils or wheat flour; the women laughed about finally being able to see their husbands now they were all locked in together, but no one ever once spared a thought for me.

I heard that Natasha offering to set up a grocery delivery service for the neighbourhood, but she didn't approach me to see if I needed any help. No one ever peeked across my wall, and no one called to wish me well. I was ignored and set aside, just as I always have been in this hateful, godforsaken place.

No. I lie. I wasn't entirely forgotten by Natasha, for one morning before the sun had even risen, the little madam came marching over the road from her home to mine. She rang the doorbell, pressing her manicured fingers on my buzzer for an eternity until all the household was up; the children, the workers who insisted on entering lockdown with us to care for the animals and every single one of the poor dogs. Rajan, who was easily roused and slept with earplugs, was woken up by the clatter too. He sat up in bed, blinking rapidly, still half asleep, and I told him I'd see what the disturbance was.

He nodded, and then said, 'What if it's a thief?'

He looked so bemused, sitting up in bed in his pyjamas, his hair ruffled, his eyes heavy with sleep, that I leant across and kissed him. The ringing continued, and he winced. 'Don't worry,' I said. 'A burglar is hardly likely to announce themselves. I'll sort this out in a minute.'

I went to the gate and saw her standing there, her finger poised before the buzzer. Her eyes were bleary, her hair a bunched-up mess, and she wore a flimsy, loosely tied pink satin robe. For a brief second, I groggily wondered if she had come over to proposition me, and then I saw her frown.

I opened the gate. There was a perfunctory apology for the noise she had made, and then she started laying into me about the dogs. She kept on screaming about how unreasonable I was being, refusing to listen to a word I had to say until, finally, I shut the gate. The infernal woman rang the bell again, and kept up the din until I opened up. She started screaming once more, threatening me with keeping a patrol outside my door, telling me she had the entire neighbourhood organised, and that they would all take turns to make my life a misery if my poor dogs didn't stop barking.

I had to lock my babies indoors then, splitting them up in various rooms around the house, robbing them of their night-time freedom. Not that she cared, the scheming bully.

I watched her home like a hawk after that, waiting for signs of her agitating against me. I watched her too, climbing up to my rooftop to get the best view, to look for signs of her slipping. Her child had local friends and I was sure that sooner or later, Natasha would invite children over, thus breaking the rules laid out by the government.

I regretted briefly not having any local allies, but really, who could interact with such low-minded people? Largely, people kept to themselves, even as restrictions were relaxed and more people were observed on the streets. People remained wary, and mingling between households was kept to a minimum. Not that I minded. No one hugged, no one socialised, and happily for me, no one went to Natasha's garden to plot against me and my four-legged babies.

Still, I kept up my vigil. And a few weeks later, I finally saw little Ms Perfect slip up.

There was noise across the road all morning long, deliveries being made from caterers and a large canopy being set up. I whistled to think of the number of people she was bringing into proximity to carry out the work, but as they remained out of doors, I couldn't reasonably object. But then, around five in the evening, as the weather turned cooler, I saw a crowd of children being ushered in through Natasha's gate. They were accompanied by parents, and in all, the gathering numbered twenty or so people. It was clearly the child's birthday; balloons were hung across the property's walls, and chairs had been laid out for a game of musical chairs.

I watched as they played games for over two hours; musical chairs and statues and pass the parcel. Music blared from loudspeakers. They were a noisy, rambunctious crowd, but when I called the police to complain, they told me that as long as the gathering was outdoors, they weren't going to break it up. I kept watching—they were consuming copious amounts of sugary drinks, and a child's bladder surely wouldn't be able to hold out for long. I willed Natasha to be the gracious hostess and refill glasses as soon as they emptied. She did. She was a whirl of energy that day, anticipating empty plates and spilt glasses and children who refused fruit but wished for more sugar. The party seemed to be a success, but I was watching out for one occurrence. And lo and behold, there it was, after the cake cutting, a sudden scramble for the indoors.

Parents lined up with their children, who stood cross-legged in their desperation. One pair disappeared indoors, and another joined the queue. Mrs Bose's daughter-in-law, who had been in the garden throughout, offered to let a child use one of the toilets in her flat. She guided them upstairs, and as she turned to respond to something Natasha said, she caught sight of me on my terrace. Her mouth first pursed and then split in a broad smile, and she waved cheerily at me before she disappeared into the building.

I waved back at her, smiling in my turn. I had more than enough evidence to back my claim. I ran to get my phone and called up the police department. They seemed bored and unwilling to take me seriously. When I insisted, they asked for evidence. 'Have you got any photos?', they said, and I heard laughter across the line. I told them that *they* were the police, that it was up to them to investigate a complaint and gather evidence, and I heard more laughter. 'Relax, madam-ji,' the man on the line counselled. 'Let the children have some fun.'

I told them they were being cavalier with a dangerous disease, and once more, the man urged restraint. 'I can't see the harm in a small gathering,' he told me. 'After all, it's been a miserable time for everyone.'

'But really, it's against the rules …'

There was a loud snort from across the line, and I could hear the policeman explain to a companion: 'It's some old busybody. Just imagine, there are people dying right now, there are people being raped, there are people stranded and losing their jobs, and here this madam is, trying to ruin some child's birthday party.'

I hung up.

Still, justice of another sort was served nearly instantly. That Natasha woman, for all the public opinion she had rallied against me, soon found that it could turn against her too.

I heard a couple of our neighbours pass comment on the evening of the party itself. Mr Rastogi from the opposite house was on the roof with the boy who worked for him as the children were being welcomed in, and I saw that he was shaking his head with disapproval. 'It's ill-judged to celebrate so publicly at the moment,' I heard him say, and I smiled. Mr Rastogi himself had been great friends with Natasha's child. Hopefully this miscalculation would bring him to his senses.

Mrs Choudhury from across the road was on her roof too, and I saw her watch the proceedings of the party. She caught my eye and I shook my head. 'A little sensitivity is called for,' I said loudly. 'People are losing their lives to this virus.'

She paused for a moment, and then nodded. She put her hands together in greeting, but didn't say anything to either agree or disagree with me. I didn't mind. She'd always been a bit aloof, that one. I saw her fan her face with her hands and wander back indoors. The sun was lower in the sky, but it remained hot. I would go in and make sure the dogs had enough water. They'd been upset by the clamour of the visit. They hated loud noises, and the minute the music had started, I had known they were sure to be distressed.

Still, despite the disturbance it had caused my poor animals, I was happy the party had taken place. It was gratifying to know that the uptight young woman who had made my life so unbearable on account of my babies would now face at least a little bit of what she had put me through. It went some way to restoring my faith in humanity to know that the fake, smiling, simpering troublemaker who had made me a pariah as she gathered the community around herself couldn't flout the rules without being held to account too.

Half A Lifetime

The email came early one morning.

Aanchal had just woken up, turning to her phone as she habitually did. She refreshed her email, not expecting to have received anything meaningful overnight, and turned her attention to the markets. They had started to recover, and she was beginning to tell clients she expected GDP to suffer no more than a 3 to 5 per cent annual fall. This was something, this change in sentiment. The earliest days of the pandemic had been dark ones for her industry, and the markets had fallen as if they had no floor, like Alice plunging into Wonderland, except the rout hadn't presaged any adventure, just misery and financial ruin.

But, and here was an example of the resilience she always urged in Sid, there had been positive stories too; the pharma and technology companies doing well as the world turned inwards, and for all the drubbing the markets had already taken, recovery was being spoken of. She was beginning to find that there were enough investors willing to bet on an upswing.

She finished checking on the markets. America had closed up overnight; a new stimulus package had been announced and the Asian markets were rallying. India would follow suit. She smiled and turned back to her email. There it was, under her news alerts and sales announcements, an email from a man she had expected to never hear from again.

Akshat Kapur. For a moment she didn't recognise the name.

Then she sighed, looking around in case Dhruv was nearby, but he was in his study, his earphones on, oblivious to her or to their son, and she turned back to her phone.

Bonjour, the subject title said.

Bonjour.

Bonjour! That is how he greeted her every morning in college, though neither of them spoke French, and though neither of them had ever so much as met a French person or watched a French movie or eaten at a French restaurant visiting Paris had been the great plan of their time together. Akshat was graduating a couple of years before her, heading to grad school in America, and they made plans to meet in Paris the summer after her own graduation.

But that was all half a lifetime ago. And yet, there it was, unread and bold on her phone screen, the familiar greeting in a foreign language from a man who had long grown unfamiliar to her.

Sid came into bed, snuggling under the covers next to her, and Aanchal put her phone down, turning towards his soft, warm body. She put her arms around him, but he was already asleep, and for a while she felt his chest rise and fall, his mouth open, his breathing hot and rapid, just like the hammering of her own heart.

Half a lifetime. That's what Dhruv had said to her when she had told him she wanted a divorce.

'But we've been together for half a lifetime,' he had said, as if that would change her mind, and all she could think of was the years she had wasted with a man who didn't enjoy the things she did—ghazals or art or a cup of ginger tea in the morning. He winced if she took a sweet biscuit from the jar to dip into her tea; he refused to eat the salads she prepared in the summer months; he refused to travel beyond visiting his parents in Pune, but when she told him their marriage wasn't working, he felt pointing out the longevity of their union was a valid justification for their remaining together.

Aanchal didn't trust herself to open the email all day. She turned to her work, denying her curiosity as if punishing herself for some past transgression, but after it was all done, the cooking and feeding and virtual working—the calls with the clients, the talking them through forms and scans and the placing of orders on online banking—she permitted herself to think of Akshat.

She found the email, fixed Sid a snack, and once he was settled at the dining table, opened the message.

Hello, she read.

That's it. I've been thinking about you through this time, wondering where you are and how you are. So hello. Hello, namaste, Sat Sri Akal, and Bonjour.

He didn't sign off. There was no clumsily worded goodbye, no trifling with *Hope you're well* or *Love* or *Best Wishes* or even the cold caress of his name, but he'd thought of her and had wanted to know how she was. She looked up to see her son studying her.

'Are you okay, Mom?' he asked.

'Of course, Beta,' she smiled. 'Why do you ask?'

'You were frowning,' he said, his brow creased with concern. 'I thought you were angry with me.'

After she tucked her son in for the night, Aanchal thought of the email again. She considered her reply, drafting a few emails in her head:

Hi Akshat, Long time no hear—too passive-aggressive.

I'm doing very well—too smug.

Thank you for your email—too impersonal.

How have you been? Are you married? Are you happy?—Too personal, too probing.

I'm desperately unhappy—too nakedly, bitterly true.

That's what Dhruv had called her the last time they had fought; bitter. They were on a Zoom call with friends, and Aanchal had been subdued. She thought no one had noticed. These were Dhruv's friends they were catching up with anyway, but one of the women had mentioned she looked drained, and had asked her if she was well.

'I know it's bad form to joke about these things at this time,' she had said, putting her glasses on to get a better look at Aanchal, 'but you're really not looking good.'

'I'm just tired,' Aanchal had replied, leaning back from the scrutiny. 'It's all the cooking and cleaning and virtual schooling while working. It gets too much sometimes.'

This led to some joshing of Dhruv, 'Help her out, yaar,' he was told. 'I've learnt how to use a vacuum cleaner,' a friend told him. 'It's the best purchase I made all lockdown, and it gives Swati a break.'

After the call, Dhruv asked her why she had made him look so bad. *Because you don't help out*, she thought. *Because you haven't taken any interest in Sid's virtual schooling. Because you disappear into your den early in the morning, holding your virtual sessions with your personal trainer there, holding your conference calls there, holding your virtual office drinks there. If you didn't come out to bathe or to eat, I could easily forget you existed.* 'It was all light-hearted,' she said.

'It's not done,' he was saying. 'Now they all think I do nothing at home.'

You don't. 'I'm sorry,' she said. 'I was put on the spot and didn't know what to say.'

It was too late. Dhruv had already worked himself up over the teasing and was convinced Aanchal had meant to make him look bad. 'Your problem,' he said, rising from his seat, 'is that you are a bitter, twisted woman who can't bear for me to be happy.'

She sent a brief reply in the end. *It's so nice to hear from you, Akshat. Are you still in New York? I've been thinking about the horrible situation there, and I hope you're well.* She didn't sign off either, and though she flirted with the idea of adding a closing line, she heard footsteps from down the hall and quickly pressed 'send'.

It was Sid, asking for water. Aanchal gave him a glass and sent him back to bed. She checked her phone and smiled. She was being silly. She had just sent the email; it was ridiculous to expect an immediate reply.

She walked to Dhruv's study and opened the door. He was still at his desk, and as he heard her enter, he put his hand up to signal he was on the phone. It was hard to tell with his earphones sometimes, but now he rose, placing a quick hand on her head as he headed out.

'Food?' she whispered, and he shook his head.

'I need to get some fresh air,' he mouthed to her. 'Leave something out for me and I'll eat it once I'm done.'

Dhruv was spending more time working than he ever had before, and for weeks Aanchal had worried that his industry was suffering. But when she talked to him, he told her private equity flourished in times of distress.

'The fall in the markets is a blessing for us,' he told her. 'We invest while others panic.'

'I thought …'

He smiled. 'It's a whole different ballgame to your retail investing.'

She decided to not worry then, even as he took calls late into the night, sleeping on the daybed in his study. He was distracted when he ate with them, his attention constantly on his phone, and when she tried to engage him in conversation, he told her he had a lot going on. She had briefly wondered if he had an outside interest, but then Dhruv had always told her she was paranoid. 'I'm sorry people enjoy my company,' he had said, and that had been the end of the conversation.

And then, Akshat's email had come in, and Aanchal told herself she was worrying about nothing. Dhruv was just sociable. It made sense for him to have friends who were female. It was all normal; it was all innocent.

I'm well. We live in Connecticut now, so are away from the worst of it. But how are you? Are you still in Delhi?

There was no explaining his use of pronoun. We. Was there a wife or girlfriend? Was there a child?

The Prime Minister appeared on TV, telling the population that Indians had to be self-reliant. *Aatmanirbhar*. They were all stuck at home, with those they loved, and with those they had once loved. And her situation, she thought, wasn't as bad as it could be. She was only in a loveless marriage, after all, but Dhruv wasn't unkind. He wasn't a wife beater. It could be worse. And yet, she kept thinking of the word the Prime Minister had kept returning to. Self-reliant. Aatmanirbhar.

I'm still in Delhi, she wrote, her finger hovering over the singular pronoun. *I'm well and I'm safe and I'm so glad you are too.*

Dhruv had started to take walks out as lockdown had eased. He would leave after eating dinner, and though she suggested for their child's sake that they join him, that they take their exercise a bit earlier to time with their son's schedule, he told her he was too busy earlier on in the day. 'I'm on back-to-back calls,' he pointed out, 'and my night-time walks are the first opportunity I have to catch my breath.'

Aanchal would sometimes watch from the gate as he walked to the end of the street, past where the guard rose to salute him, turning towards the main road that ran past the neighbourhood. She sometimes imagined he had his earphones on, but that was just her imagination. It was just her fantasising there was a way out for her through infidelity, that there was a girl somewhere, young and inexperienced, who would take her husband off her hands.

Did you ever go to Paris in the end?

There was no question about family or marriage, and Aanchal didn't reply immediately. She returned to her day, helping a client liquidate her mutual fund portfolio. Sid wanted kheer for dessert, and Aanchal took her time with the dish, cooking the rice in milk she flavoured with sugar and cardamom, blanching and slivering almonds to add on top of the mix.

As she finished her work, she heard Dhruv in the hallway. He was talking on the phone. 'I'll call you, na,' he was saying in a soft voice. 'Later.'

Aanchal nodded. *No. I still dream of it sometimes.*

That night, Dhruv had taken his beer to his den, shutting the door and telling Aanchal he was turning in for the night. Turning in, sure. He might as well have hung a Do Not Disturb sign outside the door.

There was a late-night film awards function from earlier in the year, and Aanchal knew Dhruv would be watching it. There was an actress he liked, a nubile young thing barely out of her teens, and she would be gyrating suggestively on-stage for the delectation of all of India's repressed middle-aged men.

And still, she found herself feeling sorry for him. Had his life turned out the way he had wanted? Ageing, over-worked, shut in a spare room and in a loveless marriage with a wife he felt duty-bound to stay with? He got on her nerves with his boorishness, but perhaps they had been growing apart before she had even sensed it.

And though he had never articulated it, she knew there were things about her that grated on him too. Her aversion to beer; her waking up early in the morning for yoga; her refusal to eat in the hours she was carrying out her intermittent fasting. 'Just take a day off,' he would scream. 'Discover religion, like all our mothers and their mothers before them.'

For years I didn't go, but we finally visited last year. Aanchal, it's even more magical than we dreamt of. The Jardin de Tuileries, the grand sweep of the Champs-Elysees, the wine, the food, the language! We stayed on the Left Bank, where the pavements are strewn with art and with books, and when I would go out early in the morning to fetch croissants, the streets would be empty, and Paris completely still, save for me and the workers hosing the night's dirt off the city's ancient cobblestones.

As she read the email, Aanchal was glad for Dhruv's shut door and for the distraction of the awards ceremony. Sid had been tucked into bed, and she went to the corridor to watch out for signs of movement. It was quiet in the flat, utterly still, and she returned to her room, shutting the door behind her. The laptop was on her desk, the screen still lit, and though she told herself she wanted to turn in for the night, to watch some TV, to unwind, she returned to her desk. The screensaver was on now, but she moved her mouse, and the screen flared back to glorious, miserable life, back to a description that could have once been hers. The wet, cool cobblestones had been hers to discover; the art and books hers to browse through; the wine, the French food with its wonderful, inscrutable flavours, was once hers to taste.

Aanchal shut the laptop, but remained at her desk. *We stayed on the Left Bank.* That unexplained 'we' again. *I would go out early in the morning to fetch croissants.* She felt it rising within her, the explosion, the tears, that burst of unreasonable misery, and she gave full vent to it.

Dhruv emerged from his room. She heard him pause in front of her room. She felt him apply pressure on the door handle, but he appeared to have changed his mind as she heard him move on and open the door out of the flat.

Dhruv had told her he loved her when she had asked for a divorce. As if that made up for everything, the neglect, the belching after dinner and thinking it a great jape, the turning his head anytime he saw a scantily dressed woman on the screen or the road, the refusal to celebrate her birthday or take her out for lunch or dinner. His casual, repeated undermining of her, especially when he'd had a drink or two. 'We have to think of Sid too,' he had added, as if she didn't spend all day long doing that, as if in seeking to break up an unhappy family, she was wrong to deprive their son of a father who was never there.

She slept badly. Images of Paris played in her mind all night long; the Eiffel Tower that loomed over the city, the Notre Dame that had burnt down in her absence, the India-inspired spires of the Sacré-Coeur, the bateaux-mouche winding down the Seine.

She was unsure of what more to say to Akshat, and anytime she was distracted from her work, by Dhruv laughing from down the corridor or by Sid coming in for help with his schoolwork, her mind wandered to his last email. Had he been this observant when they had been together? There had been presents, sure, and flowers plucked from spring branches for her, but she had thought those attentions symptomatic of a first love. Dhruv had been the same when they first met, opening the door for her, remembering anniversaries and birthdays, bringing home red velvet cake from the bakery in the centre of town when he passed it, but those gestures had faded over time.

She told herself that they had both got busy, with Sid, with work, with paying off the mortgage and the car loans, but there Akshat was, braving the cold Paris morning to fetch croissants. And here came the agonising conjecture—for whom? A lover, a wife, a family? A child, maybe two, a boy like Sid, or a girl, perhaps, a girl with a gap-toothed smile and long hair she wore in twin pig tails? It was torture to her to imagine the various men Akshat could have grown into. A cheat, a divorcé, a doting family man … but try as she might, she couldn't lift herself from the torment of her speculation.

She didn't reply to Akshat's email that day. His first emails hadn't required much from her; a polite interest, a fond recollection of their time together, but his last message had been hard for her to process. She told herself she'd been content enough with her life, and if she hadn't exactly been happy, she had consoled herself with the knowledge that she wasn't actively unhappy either. That was something too. It was a low-lying throb in her, her discontent. It was an old scar, and like an old scar, it was easy to ignore. She had enough, she did enough, she was loved enough, she laughed enough. It was enough.

But now Aanchal felt unmoored, though she wasn't able to articulate—even to herself—why she felt so dissatisfied. She mulled over a response for a week or longer. She kept expecting to hear from Akshat again, to have him nudge her for a response, but he didn't email, and this added to her misery. She began to wonder if she had imagined his emails, and after much agonising, she returned to her inbox to find his messages, and she found she had unearthed a fresh pool of unhappiness.

Aanchal thought of the Prime Minister's words, enigmatic as they had been. Aatmanirbhar. Self-reliant. Maybe Dhruv had chosen this route already; hiring a personal trainer without involving her, holding virtual drinks with his team and his friends on his own. They had been two moons revolving around their child for some time now, and maybe it had taken their time together in lockdown for her to realise it.

She worked through the day, making sure Sid was focused on his virtual learning, and then, as the day darkened, and as Dhruv went out for his nightly walk, she went onto the Make My Trip website. She searched for flights for two to Paris for the following summer, gasping at how affordable the tickets were in this time of introversion.

It should have passed in a year, she felt, the virus and its chaos. And even if it didn't, this imagined future still meant something. She and Sid together in Paris, for a week, for a fortnight, visiting Disneyland, gorging on crepes in Montparnasse, drinking hot chocolate with too much cream, having their portraits drawn outside the Louvre and watching the city's workers hose the night off its cobblestoned streets.

Chronicling This Time

Early on in the new academic year, they were asked to write about what lockdown meant to them. It had been a month or more since the country shut down. Mallav had forgotten precisely how long, and he thought it was typical of the time that he didn't have the concentration required to tackle his task.

'I'm not asking you to confront some heavy-duty tome,' Professor Sharma, young and new to the university, said to them. 'But chronicling this time should help keep your analytical faculties sharp.'

Analytical faculties, Mallav thought. Analytical faculties. When it was as much as he could manage to remember to shower in the morning, when it was as much as he could manage to maintain eye contact with his mother when they congregated for mealtimes, when it was all he could do to keep himself from strangling those damned mongrels next door, and when it was all he could do to stop himself from spending his entire day in the garden looking out for the mongrels' beautiful mistress.

On a Zoom call to mark a family wedding anniversary, his cousin in America asked how his writing was going. 'Well,' he said, shrugging, slouching back as his mother stared at him.

'But it's so easy for you,' his cousin said. 'I mean, your father is a famous journalist. And there is that celebrated writer opposite who is giving you feedback on your poetry, I thought.' She had just qualified as an OBGYN, his cousin, and he wondered if he could point out that her father was an OBGYN too. Had her father's profession eased her way through medical school? She was laughing now, flashing a bulbous engagement ring. 'And you have the blessing of Covid on top of everything. All you have to do is sit in your room and write. No distractions. What could be better!'

'Really,' his mother complained. 'He's hardly ever out of his room anyway. God only knows what he does all day in there,' and then it was a free-for-all, everyone chiming in with an opinion, everyone ribbing him for his slouching and poor attitude and monosyllabic replies.

An aunt snorted at Mallav's indifference. 'Oof,' she said, 'there is something wrong with this generation.' She meant her son Abhay, of course. His first cousin and two years his senior, Abhay had been pushed by his parents into a degree in economics instead of studying psychology as he had wanted to.

'It'll be too depressing,' he was told repeatedly. 'Interacting with all those unstable type people.' And so he had done as his parents advised, following up his undergraduate degree with an MBA in the UK that had cost his family dearly, in money as much as in shattered expectations, as Abhay had returned to Delhi after his studies unemployed. The outlook in the UK had been downbeat on account of Brexit, and employment visas weren't forthcoming for foreign students when so much of the existing workforce was looking for jobs.

He had remained, for the best part of three years, in a room in his parents' house in Delhi where he applied for jobs he didn't so much as receive an interview call for. His applications grew indiscriminate, and the last Mallav heard, Abhay had begun to apply to call centres who rejected him for being too old and too educated. 'I can't catch a break,' he told Mallav the last time they met. It had been at a family function, and the two cousins had snuck out to the garden to smoke a quick cigarette. 'I've been out of the job market for too long, and there are younger people graduating all the time. No one will look at me.'

'Something will come up,' Mallav had said, slapping his back, and though Abhay had smiled, and though he had nodded, they had both known his prospects weren't good.

Nothing did come up. Abhay stayed at home, becoming increasingly reclusive as time went on. Hikikomori, they called the phenomenon in Japan, referring to the youths who had responded to an unfavourable job market by withdrawing from society. Abhay put on weight, spending his evenings playing Fortnite and watching reels on his phone. He avoided socialising with his childhood friends who all seemed to have moved on in life, joining their parents' businesses, progressing in their vocations and getting married.

Abhay hadn't attended the last family wedding, and now that Mallav paused to consider, he couldn't remember the last time he had met or spoken to his cousin. Unsurprisingly, he had shied away from the scrutiny that was sure to accompany the family Zoom call, and Mallav mostly found himself wishing he had followed his cousin's example.

'You millennials!' Abhay's mother was sighing, and he had to refrain from pointing out that he and Abhay were part of Generation Z, that dreamless, zombie generation born without even the hope of the millennials, born without the euphoria that surrounded the fall of the Berlin Wall, born without the idealism that accompanied the end of the Cold War, born without the memory of India Shining to light their way to their bleak futures.

They were the generation that envied the millennials, for even though the millennials had graduated to chaos and despair, they at least had the memory of childhoods filled with hope, childhoods spent before it all turned to rot; the dream of globalism and secularism and liberalism and belonging, the hope for a brighter tomorrow for their spent, charred planet. They said he was lucky, with his well-known journalist father. But they were all folding, the print magazines, the newspapers, the bookshops, the poetry journals. The outlets that remained were all being run by the millennials and the Generation Xers who already had so much compared to their Gen Z that was last in everything, last in aspiration, last in opportunity, last in luck, last in hope, and last too in the tired, sorry alphabet.

Later, he was surprised by his sister-in-law thanking him for turning the heat off her. 'I was glad that they were so busy bullying you about your writing that they didn't bother to tell me I should be using this time to get pregnant.'

He smiled, inflating his stomach. 'I haven't been to the gym in months,' he said. 'They'll be telling me I look pregnant next.'

'The gym,' she sighed, looking out of the window. He remembered how much he had liked her the minute she had been presented as a suitable match for his older brother. She had been unassuming, had not seemed bothered as his mother informed her that her home was run by her rules, and that she was not going to make changes for a newcomer. 'Sure,' she had shrugged, not taking offence, and he had known she would be easy to get along with.

'And more than my looking pregnant,' she said as she slapped the paunch out of his stomach, 'I'm going wild sitting in the same room.' She looked at him and pursed her lips. 'I don't step out of this space apart from mealtimes. And after the first few weeks, after the frenzied Zoom calls checking on friends I hadn't thought to be in touch with for years, there's been nothing for me to do. There's no going to the office, there's no going to the kitchen,' and here she shot a quick look at Mallav, 'when your mother feels so threatened. There's no visiting my parents in Amritsar. There's nothing to do at all.'

'We can eat.'

'We can eat,' she agreed, 'but while I can't move, I find all this eating is going straight to my belly.' She stuck her stomach out so that it looked like she was pregnant under her straining kurta, and laughed as Mallav's eyes grew round with shock.

Every morning he sat down and tried to focus on his assignment: what was lockdown to him? It was being grateful, despite his political leanings, for an assertive government moving to decisively lockdown the country. It was the hoarding of all essential items—wheat flour, rice, different daals and Maggi noodles. It was the paying off of all daily workers—the guards, the drivers, the cleaners with the hope that things would be back to normal soon. It was watching from the safety of his TV screen as they walked in their thousands, India's migrant workers, walking back thousands of miles in their torn slippers and tattered clothes as the summer sun beat down on them, it was watching as they walked to distant villages in favour of starving in the cities that had suddenly turned inhospitable to them.

It was turmoil and despair and upheaval. It was mourning the tragic suicide of a talented actor. It was gang rapes and farmers' protests and cancelled exams. It was looking on in rapt disbelief as the national media turned its attention—not to defence matters or politics or the tanking economy or the spread of the virus—but to Bollywood love lives and drug consumption.

Lockdown was not writing a single word. It was not reading either, not a single book, nor a single academic article. It was telling himself he was sick to death of the endless distraction offered by the media—the prime-time media trials, the gawking at the biggest stars of the movie industry—but watching with rapt attention instead of turning to his own work.

It was watching *Normal People* and *Panchayat* and *Paatal Lok*. It was nodding politely while his mother told him to watch the re-airing of the holy epic *Ramayana* with her; it was intentionally forgetting to join her, and it was her making up for the omission by giving him a blow-by-blow account of all the action he had missed.

It was deciding not to watch *Indian Matchmaking* on Netflix until his sister-in-law made him sit down next to her; it was his rolling his eyes at the practice even as she joined in his hilarity, it was their finding the practice ridiculous and outdated until that horrid woman on TV told a young, feisty girl that her ambitions were secondary to any imagined husband's, and it was his sister-in-law falling silent and telling him she no longer felt like watching the series.

Lockdown was the crusty old man Rastogi coming out to chat to the cute little child opposite; it was Mrs Bose in her balcony watching with her daughter-in-law as the neighbourhood fitfully attempted to return to life. It was the morning and evening walks being resumed, even though no one hugged in the streets and no one ventured too close to one another.

Lockdown was also that minister claiming cow urine provided protection against Covid-19; it was the other one claiming that yoga was the answer; it was his father—who had always taught him to believe in India's secular ideal—telling him that it was a certain community, unfortunately, that had first spread the virus.

Lockdown was border skirmishes with China, and the country turning against their larger neighbour. Lockdown was the nation's media pointing out territory that had been seized by their neighbours to the north even as the Prime Minister insisted there was no trouble and that no territory had been yielded. It was the same Prime Minister announcing that Chinese apps including TikTok and PUBG were to be banned. It was people declaring they wouldn't buy Chinese made goods, without realising that all the panicked purchases they had made as the pandemic spread, all the thermometers, electric shavers, TV monitors and smartphones, were all Made in China.

Lockdown was that boorish mountebank from Republic TV who ranted on screen about Muslims, about the Chinese, and in one incredible outburst about being given drugs, drugs and more drugs. It was a mad, maddening time, and the worst was, there was no sight of it ending. They called for students to appear for college entrance exams, even as the home minister contracted the virus, even as the elite of the country—parliamentarians, businessmen, teachers—continued to conduct their business from the safety of their homes.

Lockdown was a million inaccessible memories. It was the nostalgia the time invoked in him, until Mallav found himself missing even his daily commute to college. It was missing the heat of the metro that took him to his campus;

it was missing the bus he took on the days he was running late. It was missing the thrusting elbows, the smelly armpits, the pushing and the squeezing, the jostling and the shoving, and it was missing the 'Abbe's and 'Arre's and the less salubrious warnings cast out into the morning air by the thousand other souls making their way to their working days.

Lockdown was missing life on campus. It was missing his friends, it was missing a slap on a back, a rude joke shared on Whatsapp and then repeated bawdily on sunlit college lawns, it was missing jumping out from behind a tree and scaring a passing friend. It was missing all his classmates; the girls in their strappy shoes; the boys with kurtas worn over their jeans. It was missing an afternoon spent at the food court where they lingered over steaming hot chai and a single dish of chicken lollipops. It was missing the scrambling to pool together their resources when the bill arrived, the notes, the sparkling five-rupee coins, the tallying and bartering and agreeing, the IOUs until the numbers matched.

Lockdown was missing the college library, for all the unrest it had seen in the past year with the nationalist goons breaking into the campus and thrashing students for the crime of existing. It was missing the guards at the gate who attempted to keep them safe even as the police ushered in the miscreants. It was missing his professors, who came out to speak to the press and tell them that it wasn't acceptable, in this temple of learning, to question the act of questioning.

Professor Sharma emailed him. Lectures had been held online for months now, and after the summer break, Mallav had hoped his missed assignment hadn't been noticed. And yet, there it was, late one Sunday evening, when no one had any business thinking about work, an email from his freshly minted professor about his missing project.

> Dear Mallav (wrote the Prof),
>
> I hope you are keeping well during this strange and unnerving time. I am aware that this is a trying period and all of us are facing challenges of one sort or another. Having said that, your *What Does Lockdown Mean to You* assignment was due before the summer holiday. I am sure you have found the time to complete it and that you simply omitted to email it across to me. I would very much appreciate it if you could hand it in at your earliest convenience.
>
> With kindest regards,
>
> Professor Anshu Sharma (PhD, MA, Hons (Oxon), BA, Hons (Oxon))

Mallav sat studying the email for a long time. Stange and unnerving time … simply omitted to email … earliest convenience … kindest regards … (PhD, Ma, Hons (Oxon), BA, Hons (Oxon)). He didn't know what the man was smoking, or whether Oxon was related to the oxen that ploughed the fields in rural India, but this email formed a definite highlight in the strange and unnerving time the professor wrote about.

Mallav heard the sounds of dinner being prepared in the kitchen, and leaned back in his chair. Professor Sharma wanted to see his work. He nodded, once then again. He would get to it the next morning.

She didn't venture out, the girl with the demon dogs, not in the mornings, not in the hottest hours of the afternoon, never in the hours he paced the garden, and he wondered if she was scared of being infected. But then, that evening as he went outside after dinner, he saw her. He didn't speak to her; they had never before exchanged any words beyond a cursory hello when they had passed one another, but he now nodded at her and smiled.

She didn't turn away, and his smile broadened.

This was the sighting he had thirsted for all lockdown. This was the apparition that made it all worthwhile, all the suffering, all the loss of concentration, all the nostalgia. She spoke now, telling him that she preferred not to venture outside, that they were all plebs, all the others in the neighbourhood, all unable to appreciate animal rights, he nodded happily and wordlessly, remaining mute as she told him that it was insufferable being in this miserable neighbourhood in this miserable time, even as he had never been more thankful for living when and where he did.

The Coronavirus Rhapsody

Mihir fired up his laptop and checked his email. In general, Mama didn't like him using technology first thing in the morning. 'You're better off reading a book or scanning the newspaper when you wake,' she would say to him every morning. 'Or, God forbid, having a conversation with someone in your family.'

But he didn't mind. They were all busy adjusting to the lockdown and to this increased proximity with each other. He felt for his parents, having to combine work with the home sphere, but most mornings, it was well after eight by the time Mama poked her head round his door to check in on him, by which point he would have been on his laptop for upwards of an hour.

If there was a positive to the lockdown, it was that it honed his reflexes. He was constantly on the lookout for a voice down the hall or for a footstep heading his way, when he would rapidly slam his computer shut and open his copy of *The Hobbit* to a random page.

Papa bought his subterfuge, but Mama was less easily fooled. 'I was a child before you were even born, kiddo,' she would say to him. She would check which page he was on, telling him that he was taking an age to get through the book.

'It's a long book, Mama.'

'It's not that long, Mihir. And you've been stuck on it since the start of the year,' Mama complained, arguing that given that lockdown had cut out his school commute and his leisure activities, he ought to have been getting more done, and he nodded. He did have more time on paper, and Mama was right to expect him to be productive, but what he found hard to explain to her was that the laptop she disliked so much functioned as his window into the world.

It was how he logged on to class; it was how he handed in his homework and practised his papers for the secondary school entrance exams that would take place when the new school year began. And in the absence of a phone—Mama still wouldn't buy him one—he had downloaded WhatsApp, House Party and Discord onto his laptop and used these to chat with his friends.

'Borrow my phone,' Mama would tell him. 'Use it to call one of your friends.' But she didn't understand that so much of his generation's interaction revolved around their relationship to technology. They competed in House Party quizzes together; they synced their movie consumption on Netflix Party; they watched each other play on the Xbox over FaceTime. He'd found a website called Nitro Type that helped him practise his typing, and as his words per minute count grew, he began to attract followers. They would watch on an affiliated YouTube channel as he typed out challenging passages, and when Mama, whose email account was linked to his profile, asked why he was gaining followers on YouTube, he told her the truth.

'They watch me type,' he told her as she slapped a hand against her forehead.

'They watch you type?' she asked. 'They log in from the far corners of the globe to watch a ten-year-old child type a passage out on his computer?'

'Yup.'

She mocked his generation for its love of repetitive lyrics and monosyllabic conversations. Both she and Papa despaired over his reliance on technology, worrying that he would lose his ability to hold a conversation, but what they didn't see was that this was interaction too, this watching TV at the same time as his friends, this listening to the same music and watching others play a computer game, that this provided community and belonging in a time when no physical contact was permitted.

Nanu and he had been emailing for years, but their communication was staccato in format. Nanu would come across an interesting joke or a funny video—it was invariably about animals being clumsy or cute, and Mihir often wondered if his grandfather's interests genuinely lay in that direction or if he was trying to pander to his grandchildren—and the child would reply with a comment or a meme of his own.

There were messages sent to mark birthdays, and others for festivals and holidays. But soon after the UK entered lockdown, Mihir received an email from Nanu:

Dear Mihir,

I hear you've broken up from school early. I envy you. I never had such luck as a child.

Love,

Nanu.

Mihir smiled. He knew that Nanu would never attempt to send a similar message to his younger sister Nikki, who was going through a sanctimonious phase. *Nanu*, she would have scolded in response, *people are dying*.

Dear Nanu,

I missed the end of term, which is when homework stops and we spend our final days at school watching movies. They serve us hot dogs and burgers for lunch, and the canteen staff pretend not to notice if you go back for seconds of dessert. I do miss not being in school for these days, but more than that, I miss not being able to be in Delhi with you.

Lots of love,

Mihir.

The response was all but immediate:

Dear Mihir,

You know I can never think of my favourite grandson as being mistaken, but you <u>are</u> mistaken, for though I can't hug you or take a walk with you, I wake up in the morning to a lovely message from you. I'm getting to spend time with you without all the other distractions of a visit to Delhi, and though I long to see you in person, I am so happy to be in touch with you by email.

Lots of love,

Nanu.

Dear Nanu,

You make a good point, and this is probably our longest email 'conversation'. But I hope you are taking care of your health. Mama worries that Purnima Didi will be coming in to clean and that you'll send Chetan Bhaiya to the market which will bring germs into the house. Is Chetan Bhaiya still with you or has he gone back to his family? I heard some workers were having to walk all the way to their villages.

Lots of love,

Mihir.

Mihir had turned ten during the early days of lockdown. Mama bought a whole load of balloons she and Papa blew up as he and his sister slept. Mihir's favourite cake, a chocolate and raspberry brownie, was prepared, and his best friend came round to speak to him from his front door.

Nikki wrote him a poem she proudly read out just before they cut the cake:

How to Spoil My Brother's Birthday

On his birthday my brother will think he's a king.
He'll eat all his favourite food and he won't even share,
He'll eat all his cake and he won't even care!
Then he'll play all his video games,
He'll watch his favourite tv …
… but he won't let me see!
He'll shout out orders
And say we must obey
Just because it is his day!
He will wear a crown on his head
He will make us sing …
… but that is just not my thing!

So…

I will lick the frosting off his cake!
I will open all his presents, make no mistake!
I will set the tv on Paw Patrol and not his silly show!
I will remove the batteries from his rotten games console!
I will keep him up late by making farting noises all night,
And when he says, 'Don't do that! You must obey!'
I won't listen to a word he'll say!

Now we're both in bed
Tucked up and sung to and kissed gently on the head.
'Goodnight,' says my brother,
'When I wake up, the first person I'll see,
Will be my best friend,'
And he points straight at me.

I smile then, and sigh,
As we drift off to sleep.
Tomorrow is a good day.
It is a great day.
It is my big brother's 10th birthday!

There was a lot of clapping in response, and Mihir squinted at her and asked, 'You didn't actually lick my cake, did you?' She didn't respond, but began to recite the poem out again, her hands on her hips, her enunciation growing more devilish with every line she spoke.

Later that week, Mihir wrote unbidden to Nanu:

Dear Nanu,

Can I tell you something?

Lots of love,

Mihir.

Dear Mihir,

Please do.

Lots of love,

Nanu.

PS—have you finished that lovely brownie cake? It looked delicious on FaceTime.

Dear Nanu,

We had our last slices of that cake this morning, and I can confirm it was as tasty as it looked. But now, the matter I wanted to discuss with you. Mama has been scolding me that I'm spending too much of my time online, and I thought I would ask you for your advice.

Lots of love,

Mihir.

There was no immediate reply to this and Mihir went to sleep worried that Nanu was offended by his complaining about Mama. But when he woke up, he saw a note waiting for him in his inbox.

My dear Mihir,

Mamas are always good at scolding, and when I was a child many, many years ago, I would wonder if Mamas had to take an exam in bossiness. But I'm sure you will agree that your Mama only wants the best for you.

Lots of love,

Nanu.

Dear Nanu,

I know Mama loves me and that she wants the best for me. She wants me to focus more on my reading and creative writing, and to spend less time on my computer, but I need to practise for my entrance exams for secondary schools and that is done online. I wish I could explain that to her.

Lots of love,

Mihir.

Dear Mihir,

Perhaps school exams have changed since my day, but is it really all online? Is no preparation to be done by reading or writing?

Lots of love,

Nanu

PS—I hope you're managing to get some fresh air too. Remember, all work and no play makes Jack a dull boy.

Dear Nanu,

It's a good thing, then, that I'm not called Jack! Seriously, though, after the initial online tests, I will have to go for an interview to the schools. There I will meet the heads of the schools and do more tests in Maths and English.

Lots of love (and I hope you're not having to work all day long),

Mihir.

In his next email Nanu suggested they make a deal. For every piece of writing Mihir did, Nanu would supply another. 'I haven't really written since my school days,' he told his grandson. 'Reports, sure, but no real writing since I was a teenager. But I'll be happy for you to set me writing prompts, and in return I'll set you some of my own.'

The next time they spoke, he told Mihir that he had set up a book club with a child next door. 'She's a little girl, around the same age as Nikki.'

'Is she as bossy?'

'She is,' Nanu replied. 'So, I have to behave around her. I have to read the books and tell her what I think of them otherwise she scolds me.'

The two were on the phone, using Mama's FaceTime. 'You know what the child, Navya, has called the book club?'

'What?'

'The New New Delhi Book Club.'

Mihir laughed at the sound, but Nikki, who had snuck in unannounced, nodded her head sagely. 'Of course,' she said, 'the city is called New Delhi, so the new book club has to be called The New New Delhi Book Club.'

Mihir missed his first deadline. He had homework due in at the start of the week, and had spent his free time after schoolwork on Nitro Type. Papa had begun to take him and Nikki out for walks in the neighbourhood in the evenings, and every once in a while, he and Mama would walk up to a friend's house and stand outside so they could 'meet' at a distance.

When Nanu called to remonstrate, Mihir told him he scolded him as much as his mother did. 'She *is* my daughter, Mihir. Who do you think she learnt from?'

He set the boy a challenge, to write a poem or a story taking revenge on Nikki for the poem she had written, but Mihir had another idea. 'What if I set up a website?'

'But Beta, that's more time spent online.'

'I've spent lockdown perfecting my typing skills and on exam prep. I'm sure I can create a website on my own and without any outside help. It'll be a good way to showcase my skills.'

'But …'

'I'll create it over the weekend,' he told his grandfather, and as the man looked like he was about to interrupt, he added, 'and I'll write a piece of my own choosing for it afterwards.'

Nanu still looked uncertain, so Mihir said, 'I know you're worried about my impressing the school heads at the interview. Won't it be impressive if I can say I built a website on my own during lockdown and filled it with news and pieces from this time?'

After Mihir built his website and populated it with all the news articles from the world that struck him as pertinent, he began to work on a poem. Nanu would ask him daily how he was progressing, and though he couched his queries in nonchalant language, referring to his progress on a piece or to the latest book his neighbour had given him, his inference was clear.

Mihir began to tease him with red herrings. After a fortnight of telling Nanu he was on the cusp of producing something, he sent across the following:

This Summer

This Summer,
It's a bummer,
It makes me scream
For picnics and ice cream.

There was no reaction for the rest of the day. Mama, Mihir knew, would have screamed at him if she had seen such a half-hearted production, but Nanu, when he did write to him in the morning, told him he agreed with the sentiment of Mihir's poem, and a summer without ice cream was a waste.

'I'm getting Chetan Bhaiya to cut up and freeze the season's best mangoes,' he wrote to the boy. 'And when you and Nikki next visit, you will have them served over vanilla ice cream.'

No further mention was made of the poem, but when Mihir knew Nanu had retired to bed, he sent him the poem he'd actually been working on all week.

Coronavirus Rhapsody
(in the style of *Bohemian Rhapsody* by Queen)

Call it corona,
or Covid-19,
Locked up at home,
I call it an altered reality.

Open the windows,
Look out at the sunshine, daydream …

I'm just a bored boy,
From a bored family.

Because you sneeze into your elbow,
Do not cough, blow that nose!

Even just a small cough will make no one come near to me,
to me …

Mama, need another tissue,
Too many days being wasted,
Not many doses now left

Of Piriton, that minty medicine,
But now Covid-19's ruining all our days.

Mama, oooh
Didn't mean to make you cry,
If I have the bug this time tomorrow,
Carry on, carry on,
As if nothing really matters.

Too late, my time has come.
I can feel my heavy breathing,
Got that hot temperature feeling.

Goodbye, everybody, I've got it now.
Gotta face the pain and take it with good attitude.

Mama, oooh,
I don't want this bug,
I sometimes wish I'd never been born at all …

(guitar solo …)

I see Sky News morning to afternoon,
Lots of cases, lots of deaths, lots of action!
Lockdown extended, very, very frightening to me!

Very scary (high voice)

Very scary (low voice)
Very scary (high voice)
Very scary (low voice)
Very scary (high voice)
Very scary, yes indeed (low voice)

How are we surviving-ing-ing-ing?

I'm just at home,
Nothing to do at all.

He has just nothing to
do while he's at home.

Have mercy for him, Covid-19!

Please, oh please, Covid-19 will you save me now?

Bismillah! No, I will not save you now! (save him now!)
Bismillah! I will not save you now! (save him now!)
Bismillah! I will not save you now!

Save me now! (will not save him now!)
Save me now! (will not save him now!)
Save me now-ow-ow-ow-ow!

No, no, no, no, no, no, no!

Oh mamma mia, mamma mia!
Mamma mia save me now!

Coronavirus has it specially put aside for me, for me, for me!!!

So you think I will lie down and let you take my life?!

So you think I will give up with one tiny sigh?!

Yes covid, not so weak, covid.
Just gotta fight this,
Just gotta fight this bad disease.

We can fight this virus, anyone can see …
We can fight this virus …
We can fight this virus …
You'll see ...

Nanu replied within the hour.

My dearest Mihir,
This was absolutely brilliant. Wow. Just wow.
Yours in awe,
Your proud Nanu.

Mihir smiled. His mother came into his room and put an arm around him. 'Have you done all your homework, baby?'

'Yes, Mama.'

'I've made you a fruit salad. Finish it off and then you can go out for your walk.'

He nodded. 'I just have to finish one thing, and then I'll come.'

She squinted at him. 'Mihir, sweetie, I really do think you're getting addicted to that laptop of yours.'

'I'm not,' he said, smiling even as she continued to frown. 'Just give me a minute. I have an email to send to Nanu.'

'Nanu?' she asked, surprised, then nodded.

Mihir waited till his mother had left the room before loading the email he had started to compose to his grandfather. He smiled. Nikki would approve of the message. He was going to introduce her to Nitro Type the coming weekend. He wanted her to make use of this time and get completely familiar with the keyboard. The website held competitions too, with virtual rewards for fast typing speeds, and he knew this was just the way to incentivise his younger sister to achieve. Mama would complain, but it wasn't all bad, the time he was spending on the computer.

Dear Nanu,

While I'm thrilled you've enjoyed the poem (and I really am), I worry you're spending too much time on your computer. Don't you think you should go to sleep?

Lots of love,

Mihir.

He rose as Mama called out to him, and shutting his laptop, made his way out to where his family waited.

Black Lives Matter

They're all coming out to protest in the streets now with their T-shirts and their placards and their earnest, tear-stained faces. All the enthusiastic, idealistic children from down the street, and the rest of the neighbourhood with them. All the earnest faced eco-warriors, all the protectors of Delhi's mongrel dogs, all the power-walking aunties, all the temple addicts and all the ageing, sombre-faced retirees too.

'Black Lives Matter,' they chant, even as they continue to slather Fair & Lovely cream on their faces every morning.

They're good at protests, these Indians. They are good at complaining about injustices meted out to them, even as their great leader, their Mahatma, still then on African soil, complained about Indians being treated the same as the Africans by the British, in that, the land they all sucked raw for their profit.

At the diplomatic queue in immigration, I'm stopped as the European arrivals are waved through with folded hands and a bobbed head. Do they think I can't see? Do they think I don't notice, that I don't understand the lilting, servile imitation of English that comes out of their bootlicking mouths?

'What is your business here?' I am asked, even as the people before me had their passports stamped without question. My ticket stub is examined carefully, as if to confirm that I flew First Class, that I, in my black skin, could be admitted to its air conditioned, champagne swilling confines.

I stand up a little straighter. 'I,' I tell the man in my boarding school English, 'am the wife of the Nigerian Deputy High Commissioner.'

His eyebrows shoot up and his head moves from side to side. They're still the same backward, superstitious people, temple worshippers, snake charmers … I hold my hand out for my papers. 'Welcome to India,' he says without smiling.

Years ago, my niece Precious had occasion to travel to Delhi from London. One of her friends, an Indian girl, was getting married, and a whole load of her friends had travelled for the festivities. Precious had gone too, staying with the boy she was with—a tall, strapping white lad called Angus. She later told me they pointed at her in the streets, slack-jawed like monkeys, until she averted her face and walked away.

'Black Lives Matter,' they tell me.

They knock on my door now, when the pandemic is months into its work, telling the house boy Paul that it is dreadful what is happening in America, with George Floyd, with that horrendous President in that horrendous torn-apart country, and I tell him to hold his head up high, to fold his hands together in the Indian manner and to thank them for their wishes.

They go away happy, then, and tell everyone in their social media feed that they spoke to the Nigerian Deputy High Commissioner, that he thanked them for their support, that he opened the door to the house himself and that he wore slippers and shorts like he was some common little servant boy.

Making Memories

Early on in lockdown, a clip emerged of a man making a Negroni. I can't remember now how I came across it, if I found it through my newsfeed or on Twitter. Though he was famous, I didn't recognise him, and he spoke with such authority on provenance and ratios and the only brand of vermouth it was permissible to use, and on the best glasses to use when serving the drink, that I took him for a bartender. He was bald and olive skinned and wore a tight black top and black jeans with a belt, and I thought, a man wearing a belt during lockdown! It emerged the bartender was no bartender but actually a Hollywood actor of Italian extraction, but he cast a spell over so much of the world with that clip, and now that I think of it, it was his assurance that we sought. His confident knowledge, his mastery of a drink we hadn't had in months, the harking back to a time when it was normal, commonplace even, to walk into a bar and be served a drink by a man in a black t-shirt and a pair of trousers held up with a belt. We had been reasonable to expect our drinks, we had been unexceptional in expecting them to be prepared well, and now that we could no longer expect the same, the video starring the actor I didn't recognise reminded me of what had once been pedestrian and no longer was.

What is now normal is the claustrophobia of our days. I don't mean the being stuck indoors, though that too is a drag. What I mean is that for years, my working week ran from Monday to Wednesday, and on Thursdays and Fridays, my home was my exclusive preserve.

I'd prepare breakfast and do the school drop-offs, but after that, I'd do as I pleased. I'd go out for a coffee with a friend; I'd speak to Papa over FaceTime. I'd read a book in the rocking chair in the living room, moving the chair to catch the afternoon sun; I'd snack on the chocolate digestives that were forever being polished off by the children over the weekends. I would soak daal for the evenings; I would put on a leisurely load of laundry. On days when I had to work on a deadline, I would choose where to work based on where the light was most favourable—the little desk in my bedroom in the afternoons, and the large kitchen table in the mornings where I could spread out all my papers without bothering anyone.

Now, of course, someone is always in the way. Mihir flits between his desk and the one in my room, while Nikki prefers to tackle her worksheets at the kitchen table. Sameer has his office to retreat to, and it is only if I have any energy left after I set the children up for school, print all the school papers, check all their homework, provide three meals a day and wipe down the tables for the next day's schooling that I am able to tackle my day's work. We are forever running out of clean sheets and socks and shorts, and though they don't complain, Sameer or the children, I sometimes wish they said *something* about how much this time has loaded onto my plate.

I ask Sameer what he misses most about life before lockdown, but he refuses to play the game. He views my question as frivolous, I suppose. He looks at the world with his scientist's phlegmatic approach, and tells me I'm torturing myself needlessly.

'Who knows when we'll be able to return to normal. What you're doing only makes it worse.'

Papa joins me, though, and every morning, when I call, I ask him, 'So what's on the wish list today?'

'Rasgullas from Gopala's Dairy.'

'You wished for that yesterday.'

'Did I?' He pauses as he thinks, humming on the line, just as he used to when checking through my homework. Mmmm-mmmm, a sound I've forever associated with suspense, with not knowing if I've passed or been found wanting. 'Mmm,' and then, 'deep fried paranthas from that old street, remember?'

'That old street?'

'Haan, baba, paranthe wali gali.'

Paranthe wali gali. A memory rises from the recesses of my mind. How those fat old men in their string vests would labour over the bubbling hot karahi of oil, throwing in their paranthas stuffed with radish, or a tangy potato mixture, paneer, or any item really, savoury or sweet, they could think of to stuff between two disks of rolled out dough. The closeness of the street, the smells, the noise, the filth. 'Papa,' I cry. 'The entire world is reassessing how it lives its life, and here you are, dreaming about those filthy paranthas?'

'Seriously,' he replies, and I can almost see him smile. 'When will we ever have those pleasures again?'

'With any luck,' I say primly, 'never.'

I dream of the pasts motherhood has denied me. The unhurried weekend brunch with friends, the stroll through a sunlit park without having to worry about mealtimes or playgrounds or bursting bladders. A hug, a compliment on a new dress or on a tan or a perfume, and then that unrushed, unpressured togetherness of time spent together in the certainty that it can be reprised at a moment's notice. An exhibition at the National Gallery; a train ride to Paris to take in the Orsay. A pair of towering stilettos purchased in the sales, not for utility but for the sheer whimsy of the purchase. I miss the trips to the park with the children too, and the picnics, and the visits to the sea, but most of all, I miss this, the life I had before I became a grown up.

'You know what I miss?'

'What, Papa?' We have just had a mini altercation. I bought him a UV steriliser which he refuses to use because it was made in China. Relations between the two countries are at a low; Chinese troops have entered Indian territory in the north of the country and claimed some of our land, and even though the Prime Minister assures us that all is well, that no one is able to so much as dream of an assault on our sovereignty, the national mood has turned. Anti-China sentiment is at an all-time high. People take out TVs—Chinese made, of course—and smash them on the streets. Papa refuses to use the steriliser because it is made in China, and I don't have the heart to tell him that everything is now made in China, our phones, our batteries, even the paracetamol tablets we are turning to during the pandemic. I'm grateful when he switches the topic of conversation, and I repeat my question: 'What, Papa?'

'Your childhood.'

'My childhood?'

'Yes,' he replies. 'I've been lending some of your old books to Navya, the child next door …'

'I hope you're taking care …'

'Ohho, I am. Now listen.' He clears his throat, and I wonder for a moment if he is coming down with something. 'I miss reading books to you. Amar Chitra Kathas, the Panchatantras. I miss taking you for a walk to the park in the evenings. I miss that trip to Appu Ghar.'

'Appu Ghar,' I say, remembering. 'That old junk yard …'

'You scoff now,' he says, his voice soft, 'but how it thrilled us all back then. You clamoured to go on all the rides and wouldn't let us leave until the park was closing for the day. We bought you candy floss and you made us queue to have your name written—do you remember?—your name written on a grain of rice.'

'Of God, yes,' I say. 'I still can't imagine how he did it.'

'I have it, you know.'

'The vial with the grain of rice?'

'Yes,' he says. 'You must have left it among your things when you went off to England, and your Mama must have retrieved it. I found it in her jewellery box the other day.'

After all this is done, he'll come over to England, and we will go to an amusement park. Legoland, which Mihir has nearly outgrown, or the Chessington World of Adventures some of his friends have already visited.

They'll go on one of the rollercoaster rides, grandfather and grandson, while Nikki and I search for one of the water rides. They'll have too much sugar, of course, an ice cream for a treat, and then another on account of the heat, and by the end of the day they will all be overstimulated and teary, grandfather and grandchildren, and I will be hot and thirsty and tired. I will have spent my day carrying bags and bottles of water and sun hats and sunglasses and sun cream and negotiating between a child who wants pizza and another who wants a burger. I will be teary too, though no one will think of asking me how I am until I erupt.

I will tell myself I will never put myself through the hassle again, that my children are savages, but in the morning, as they all come before me with their shining faces and their large, enveloping hugs, I will nod as they tell me what a wonderful time they had. They will ask if they can go to the park again while their grandfather is still visiting, they will promise to behave, and I will tell them yes, of course, we will all go, and their father too, we will all go as a group and make the memories I will return to when it has all passed.

Better Safe Than Sorry

Jeet Bhaiya had loaned me the money to buy the house back in 1985. Loaned, I say, even though he refused to let me repay him. He had inherited his money as the older son of an older son, properties falling the right way over generations, and when he received his windfall on the death of his father, he sold his properties in the village and invested in a wholesale business in Sadar Bazaar.

I still worked as a trainee accountant in those days. The idea was for me to finish my qualification before I began to pay Jeet Bhaiya back, but he suggested an alternative. He was just setting up his business, and my skills, he told me, would be invaluable to him. He offered me a role at nearly twice the salary the accountancy firm paid me. He would cut the money I owed him from my salary until my debt was repaid. I agreed, and took a share in the business, but my salary was paid whole to me, and though Jeet Bhaiya claimed he deducted part of it in recognition of my debt, I was never once out of pocket.

For years, Ma had argued that joining Jeet Bhaiya was a bad idea. 'All of India is studying engineering and medicine,' she told me. 'They're choosing such good professions, stable jobs. And you? You opt to sit in a shop with wholesalers and scrap traders …'

Ma was the widow of a younger son, and as such, had a native distrust for the older child's authority.

'But Ma,' I reasoned, 'this is better than a job. Jeet Bhaiya is giving me a share in the business.'

'A share.' A loud sniff followed. 'Why would he do that when he doesn't have to? Why would he do that when his father didn't think to provide for yours?' And then she would revert to her usual refrain. 'And electrical goods? TVs, fridges are all well and good, but they're not a regular purchase. You buy them once when you marry, and then you replace them when your children marry. Who is going to keep buying your products? And these electric shavers and your electric waxing kits; who needs them? Who is going to buy your vacuum cleaners and dishwashers when a domestic help can do the same job for you and for cheaper? The boy is throwing generations of hard-earned wealth down the drain. And you're helping him!'

Whatever Ma's early reservations had been, Jeet Bhaiya's choices proved inspired during lockdown. The men of the country's middle class households were suddenly occupied with maintaining their beards; women, struggling without the assistance of their regular domestic workers, looked for good deals on vacuum cleaners, and we found we couldn't keep up with the demand. Electric thermometers were the first to run out of stock as national hypochondria set in, then headsets and laptops and iPads, beard trimmers next, and finally, as realisation dawned that the lockdown was an indefinite provision, dishwashers and vacuum cleaners began to fly off our shelves.

We hadn't been to the shop in months. Though our business focussed on the wholesale market, supplying stores and showrooms their stock, we found that we all adjusted to working virtually. Orders came in through email, slowly at first and then with such speed that we had to try and establish alternative supply chains. We'd always sold branded European products, but now we liaised with a Chinese supplier whose products were a good third of the price.

Business was good, but I could tell Jeet Bhaiya was not happy. 'It's like a jail in here,' he complained, and I knew what he meant. After years of an established routine where we would spend our days in the shop, suddenly we couldn't step out. We were all around each other, Usha, the children and I. I should've felt lucky but couldn't help thinking that there was no escape from each other. I was unable to so much as have a minute to myself. I felt sure it was the same with Jeet Bhaiya.

Usha seemed to have welcomed lockdown, and tried to fold our routines into her own. Tea and breakfast were prepared in the morning, as always, but now the rest of the day's rhythms lay in her control too. We ate when she deemed it to be lunchtime. I was served my tea at precise times; at eleven in the morning, and then at four in the afternoon. There was no sending the office boy out for a cup whenever the feeling struck. There was no calling in of clients or of friends. There was nothing but Usha and her fixed routine, and no escape from it either. Abha and Anuj, at least, were able to lock themselves in their rooms, and Usha didn't try to breach their privacy. 'Have to give them their privacy?' she told me, apparently without irony. And yet, when I so much as picked up my phone, there she was, her head round the door, asking me who it was I was speaking with, asking which biscuits we should next have, asking if I wanted rotis from the tandoor or the stove for my lunch.

'There's no getting away,' Jeet Bhaiya said to me. 'Sunita doesn't even let me step out onto the veranda in case I catch the virus.' I laughed, and he added bitterly, 'Tell me this. Is this virus a kung fu champion? Is it going to climb up the walls, break through the fence and then come flying at me? She's got me taking the air on the roof in the afternoon heat because she thinks that's safer. I go round and round in circles for a half hour before she lets me back down. I would give anything to be able to escape to the market.'

'Usha thinks it's a holiday.'

'Holiday? Holiday? It's pure hell in here,' said my cousin. 'We're stuck indoors when there's a fortune to be made. Do you know, we received orders for two dozen dishwashers today? And that's just for one shop. Dishwashers in India, can you imagine? And we're stuck at home.'

I felt the pull too, even though I was allowed the freedom of my veranda. I went there early in the morning after my first cup of tea. The fan there worked lethargically, but I was grateful for its presence in Delhi's stifling heat. I was grateful for the shade of the awning too, and began to read my morning papers there. It was something, some relief from the tedium of the house. Sometimes I would see Niharika next door and she would dip her head in a shy namaste, the child I had seen grow up through the years, the girl I had given *mithai* from the market on Diwali and on exam results day. It still took me by surprise to see her as a grown woman. She lived alone now that her parents had passed away some years ago, and though she was always polite, she moved indoors almost as soon as she saw me.

'She's nervous about the virus, poor thing,' Usha said.

There were others too; the retired newsman, the former bank manager, workers out on errands, housewives in their summer whites. I glimpsed life from the relative comfort of the veranda, and though I was grateful for that little insight into the world, I still missed the hustle-bustle of the market.

For all the lack of space in the shop, for all the files, the samples and the boxes, it represented freedom. This was where we felt the pulse of India's consumers. This is where we saw what our competitors were stocking, and where we saw what the nation's retailers—the family-run pharmacies, the street corner markets, the airconditioned supermarkets—were ordering. This was where deals were made over endless cups of sweet tea. This was where Jeet Bhaiya and I shared our hopes for the family, and our fears. This was where we salivated over the latest young thing to have made it in Bollywood, and though we met with our families too, it was there, in that cramped office cum shop in Old Delhi, that we were able to speak openly.

'I'm going in,' Jeet Bhaiya told me late one afternoon in May.

I could hear him pant, and knew he was on the roof for his allotted half an hour of exercise. 'I wish you luck in trying to get Sunita Bhabhi to agree.' I myself was in the study behind the kitchen, speaking in a whisper for fear of Usha overhearing me. It was a thought, though, Jeet Bhaiya in the market soon, and if all went well, perhaps I could follow. All around the world, things were starting to return to normal. They were talking of playing sports again in New Zealand. They spoke of opening bars and restaurants in Europe and in America. Life would return to normal in India too, surely.

Jeet Bhaiya ventured to the market a week later. He called me up from outside the jalebi seller's stall. 'Can you smell it?' he asked me, 'the frying oil, the sugar syrup, the sacred air of freedom?'

'You lucky thing.'

'That I am,' he laughed. 'That I am.'

Some semblance of normality began to return to the neighbourhood. One morning as I took to my veranda, I saw Shami Rastogi walking in the lane below.

He waved as he approached.

'How nice it is to see you,' I said, my smile warm.

'You too,' he smiled. He stood outside my gate and folded his hands together in greeting. He didn't look to come in and I didn't ask. 'It feels so good to see these familiar faces and these familiar homes that I can almost believe the last few months were nothing more than a nightmare.'

'But where's Smita Khanna, your walking partner?'

'I haven't seen her in a while.' He paused to recollect, then shrugged. 'We're all our own islands now.'

The Nigerian couple passed by, nodding slightly as they saw us. 'Namaste,' I called, cursing myself for having forgotten their names. Niharika would know. I would ask her the next time I saw her.

'But you're keeping well?' Shami was asking.

'Yes,' I replied, 'all things considered. I just want life to return to normal.'

'Be patient,' he counselled as he set off on his walk. 'Things are slowly getting better.'

Three days later, Jeet Bhaiya felt weak. He developed a cough, felt lethargic, slept for the majority of the day. He shivered through the night, refusing to let his wife switch on the AC. In the morning, she called the doctor. Years of sitting in the shop meant he was overweight and suffered from diabetes, and when she described his symptoms, the doctor immediately wrote out a prescription for a Covid-19 test.

She called Usha with an update, and to warn her against letting me out. 'It's probably nothing,' she told my wife, though Usha told me she cried as she spoke. 'It's just a reaction to the excitement of the market, I am sure. I'm expecting the test to come back negative, and for the maharaja to take to bed with an acute case of indigestion.'

The test didn't come back negative. Jeet Bhaiya had contracted Covid-19, presumably from the rush of the market, where, as we learned, he had followed his jaunt at the jalebi stall with golgappas and chole-bhature from the vendor next door, and then paan from the stall near the motorway. The food vendors were all doing a roaring trade. Hundreds of shopkeepers had been released after weeks of captivity, and their first instincts had been to indulge their twin loves of forbidden fruit and the buzz of the market.

The weather had been hot, he had refused to wear a mask, and all the food he had consumed had been prepared in close quarters by perspiring men. By the time he returned home, his wife estimated, he had rubbed shoulders with a hundred people in close surroundings.

It was an odd sort of comfort to think that Jeet Bhaiya was given preferential treatment on account of his pre-existing condition. He was moved to the hospital the day after his diagnosis and monitored day and night. No one was allowed to visit him, not his cousins, not his siblings, not his wife or children.

We set up a WhatsApp group called *Beating Corona*, as if this was a great adventure, a challenge or a test, and if we believed enough, if we studied or prayed hard enough, Jeet Bhaiya would recover. We were able to smuggle in an iPad; Jeet Bhaiya's daughter knew a doctor at the hospital, and we were able to be in contact. This was a comfort to him as much as it was to his family.

He responded to his anti-virals, took his paracetamol as mandated by the pretty nurses who visited him every hour. He had felt cloistered at home, but in the hospital, confined as he was to his bed, he felt fussed over and petted, and no longer spoke with wistfulness of the market.

He told me his wife had jumped the gun. It had been a little fever. There had been no need to have him hospitalised. 'Think of this as a holiday,' I told him as he snorted. He coughed in response to his action, then told me he was fine. Some water had gone down the wrong way.

'I'm sure we're all overreacting,' I told Jeet Bhaiya, 'but I'm glad you're getting proper care. You can laugh about it when you're safely back at home.'

I had taken over the handling of the business. Usha banned me from going to the market, and even though I told her I would be more careful, she told me it wasn't in my nature. 'You'll be like a freed animal,' she said. 'You'll want to visit your old haunts. You'll want to mark your territory. That's what got your stupid cousin in trouble.'

A week after Jeet Bhaiya was admitted, he looked to be improving. His cough had cleared, his fever had broken, and when I spoke to him on FaceTime, he appeared restless.

'Don't tell me you're tired of your pretty nurses.'

'I've had enough,' he told me, 'of all this bland food and this square room. I just want to go home.'

They spoke of releasing him in a day or two, and though Jeet Bhaiya demanded they expedite the process, telling me I was being over-protective, the rest of the family and I agreed it made sense to be cautious. He'd been cavalier with his diabetes. We'd known of people with conditions—a prior heart attack, asthma, diabetes—who hadn't been as fortunate as Jeet Bhaiya after contracting Coronavirus.

'It's better,' I said to Sunita Bhabi when I spoke to her, 'to be safe than sorry.'

For days I hadn't been to the veranda. There was all the worry over Jeet Bhaiya, then the handling of the business' affairs, and I found I hadn't had time to take the air. It was a good week after Jeet Bhaiya's hospital admission that I went out into the veranda.

It was hot; the sun piercing and colourless. There was no breeze, nor any moisture in the air, and the fan overhead creaked arthritically. A stupor came over me, and I found myself rereading lines in the newspaper without comprehension. This was what a stay in hospital must feel like; the same visits, the same conversations without change, a permanent sense of déjà-vu.

I must have fallen asleep, as I woke with a start. I heard voices outside, and for a brief, unthinking moment, I thought we had visitors. I walked groggily to the gate, wiping the dribble off my chin, when I saw the world was the same as the one I had closed my eyes to; Jeet Bhaiya still in hospital, the world still in lockdown, my movements still restricted, and it was only Niharika from next door conversing with a strange man. I blinked, trying to identify him, but I had never seen him before, and Niharika had spotted my attention as she lowered her voice and turned away from my gaze.

I made my way back indoors.

The reversal came a couple of days later.

Jeet Bhaiya's vitals had all been improving, and though his daily Covid-19 tests still came back positive, he had been feeling increasingly energetic when his breathing grew laboured. The change occurred late in the evening, and Jeet Bhaiya had been so eager to return to his life that he had held off complaining.

Sunita Bhabi later said he had appeared drained at their daily call but otherwise happy, and in the family chat that evening, she had told us that he was turning in early. *It's finally catching up with him*, she told us. *All the excitement of the last few days, and he just needs a good night's sleep.*

By morning, it was clear that his condition had deteriorated. His breathing grew more tortured, he found speech an effort, and his chest felt constricted, as if someone was sitting on it.

By the end of the day, he was being given oxygen.

By the end of the night, he was intubated.

Usha and I called Sunita Bhabi, who told us the hospital was still not allowing her to visit. 'They tell me the situation is very serious,' she told us. 'I should pray for him, they said.' She laughed shrilly. 'As if I've been doing anything else. I haven't been able to see him, I haven't been able to wipe his brow or massage his shoulders or take his temperature or give him a cold compress. I haven't been able to do anything that I would want to do for him. All I have done this week is prayed to a God who seems too busy to listen to me.'

'It'll be fine, Bhabi,' I said, feeling the inadequacy of my words. 'Have some faith.'

Faith. Faith, it seemed wasn't enough. Not for Jeet Bhaiya, who died on his own. Not for Sunita Bhabi, who could only see her husband breathe his last over the ipad, who had to stand alone outside as the last rites were performed in the baking heat while the rest of the family wasn't even allowed to go to the crematorium. Not for all of us on our *Beating Corona* WhatsApp group. No amount of bravado or faith or belief or prayer had been enough for any of us.

The next morning, I went out to the veranda. It had rained a little overnight, and the air was cool, the ground full of the smell of reawakening. I thought of the calls I had been receiving from our purchasers. They had expressed their regrets at Jeet Bhaiya's passing and then, hesitatingly, had told me that the sales of our Chinese products were falling. People were choosing to buy the more expensive European stock. No more of the Chinese made goods were to be ordered. And here our warehouse was, full to the rafters with new shipments. I thought of what Jeet Bhaiya would have done. He would have cut prices, arguing that Indians couldn't resist bargains. He would have struck deals with Amazon and Flipkart; he would have spoken to foreign purchasers who wouldn't have been averse to Chinese goods. He would have known what to do.

I heard Niharika in conversation next door, and though I didn't know the voice that answered back, I assumed it was the man I had seen a few days ago. He had a nice voice, soft and energetic, and I was glad Niharika had someone to keep her company. She had always been a quiet girl, shy and bookish and obedient. Too obedient, perhaps, I had thought, but now, as I heard her laugh in the clean morning air, I was glad for her happiness.

We were to hold a prayer meeting for Jeet Bhaiya in the afternoon. The priest who was to conduct the service had adapted to the circumstances, circulating invitations to a Zoom call, and sending emails with the incantations we would have to utter. It gave me comfort in this strange, bereft time to print out and read through the material. It gave me something to do, an activity at a time when I had been unable to hug a fellow mourner, when I had been unable to contribute or to organise or to help relieve Jeet Bhaiya's widow's burden. I kept the papers I printed out by me, running my fingers through them even as I avoided the morning papers, and they gave me comfort, a sense of continuity, to see the familiar prayers I had recited at the loss of every loved one; parent, in-law, aunt, uncle, cousin, and to know that this remained the same even as everything else around me was turned on its head.

The Handshake

I don't mean to be ungrateful. Really, I don't. There are mothers I know who are doing all the heavy lifting the lockdown has necessitated. The pandemic has put the cause of gender equality back a few decades, at least, and everywhere I can think of, in urban and rural India, on American farms and in liberal Europe, it is the mothers who are juggling housework, childcare and employment.

Even that Navya Singh's mother from the park side of the street, that pretty, smiling thing, even she has stopped her paid work so that she can focus on her child. 'I don't know what I would have done,' she tells me when she calls me at the start of lockdown, 'if I worked in the sort of role that had carried on as all this began.' And Navya is a good child, always respectful in class, always engaged. What do mothers with hyperactive kids do? What do mothers with two do, or those with three?

I, mercifully, have no one to cater to but myself. There is no husband. There are no in-laws, no elderly parents, no children. The minute lockdown commenced, I was able to organise my supply chains—Mrs Singh placed a call, and the Sikh grocer from the market began to deliver supplies twice a week.

For weeks I haven't stepped out of the house. No one has entered either, not a friend, not a neighbour, not a domestic worker. In some ways, I am grateful that Ma has passed. She, with her heart condition, would have been a sitting duck. Then too, she would not have taken heed of the restrictions. She would have gone out into the garden every day, even in those early, fraught first weeks when we functioned more on prayer and superstition than on any tangible science. She would have chafed against the restrictions; she would have insisted on driving out to the park to take her morning walks as she had always done. She would have been garrulous and suspicious and convinced it was all a conspiracy, and my telling her the danger was real would only have incensed her.

And yet, if she had been here, she would have been a physical presence. A body of flesh and bone, someone to worry over, someone to fight with, someone to hug or scold or laugh with, someone to be with. It's hard to explain it to anyone not in my position. For all I can feel for their stretched resources and money worries; for all I can empathise with the claustrophobia of their existence, it is hard to explain to them that I haven't touched a single person since March.

I haven't shaken an acquaintance's hand. I haven't patted a child on their back for doing well in their spelling test. I haven't sat next to someone in a car or on a metro carriage. I haven't pulled anyone back from a speeding car. I haven't given a friend a high five; haven't slapped their back at a good joke. I haven't hugged a friend or a relative. I have had no human contact since lockdown commenced.

And yet I count myself lucky. Teaching is one of the recession proof professions: children continue to need an education even as the economy nosedives. We shut the school early, and for the first few months there were no classes and no interaction with the children. But as soon as the new school year began, virtual schooling did too, and I had to learn how to give my attention to a room of thirty children when they all fit onto the screen of my laptop.

But it's provided opportunities too, virtual schooling. I've had to quickly familiarise myself with Microsoft Teams and Google Meets and SeeSaw. I notice more now, the colour of the turban on little Jai's head as the day changes, the flowers Ashna's mother arranges on the desk next to the child's laptop, the trail of a chiffon dupatta as a woman—a mother, an aunt—enters the child's frame. In this manner, I glimpse life. And on the days that Navya is seated outside on her veranda for her lessons, her little wooden table positioned next to their lemon tree, then it is as if I can reach out and touch my past, the walks on the street, the park we played badminton in as children, the sharp citrus smell of the tree on hot summer evenings.

We are so connected now; by phone and Facebook and Zoom and good old email, across geographies and time zones. Ashima checks in every week and complains she spends her days scolding people across time zones—her children in London and her father across the road from me in Delhi.

'I can scold you too, if you want,' she tells me. 'Tell me, are you eating well? Are you taking your Vitamin C and Zinc supplements?'

And when Zohra, who had been the editor of the school magazine, emails to suggest the old editorial board reconnect over Zoom, I tell her it is a good idea.

The old editorial board. It had been six of us, or maybe eight. Yes, it had been eight; six of us from the eleventh grade, and then the two veterans in the twelfth who had helped run the magazine the previous year.

I was in charge of events; mainly covering annual days, house plays, sports days and the rituals surrounding graduation—the official and unofficial parties, the fashion shows, the music contests. Pranav, the twelfth grader assigned to help me cover my beat, had been in charge of the section the year before. 'You've got the cushiest job,' he told me. He was tall and athletic and wore long-sleeved shirts he rolled halfway up his arms. His floppy hair fell over his eyes, and he spoke in a lazy, slow drawl inspired by American westerns, which I took to be not an affectation but an insight into his innermost soul.

He accompanied me to all my events, introducing me to organisers, feeding me my opinions and tastes, sliding into the seat beside me and into my dreams at night. I could imagine him lying on a hay bale in rolled up jeans, a cigarette in his mouth and a cowboy hat shading his eyes. I could imagine him herding cattle; I could imagine him crooning a slow, sad song as the sun set across distant mountains; I could imagine him draw his gun and shoot a villain dead at ten paces. He was the first boy I spent any real amount of time with, the first boy who spoke of leisure and art and desire, and I thought he was the most beautiful thing I had ever seen.

I begin my Zoom call routine. Smart top, hair freshly washed and blow dried, nail polish and make-up. It's funny how we pay attention to these details even if they may not be visible to others in the couple of square inches we are permitted on screen. I myself have shifted to wearing more dramatic make up to make myself stand out more; shifting from my peach lipsticks to berry stains.

'It makes you pop,' Zohra smiles from across the oceans.

Pranav is late for the catch up, and I remember he was always late when we were at school too. Late for assignments, late for concerts and for assemblies, and always with an excuse ready. His car would break down, the school bus would encounter traffic, torrential rain would fall between his home and the school, and half the fun of listening to his excuses was listening to the improbable details he invested them with.

We are catching up; Nisha is telling us about how worried she is about her pregnant sister at this time, when Pranav pops up on the screen. 'It's so good to see you guys,' he says, squinting. 'How long has it been?' and we laugh to tell him we have just been through this, that we have just counted the years and the divorces and the children and that he is late as he always was.

'The dog,' he asserts, 'ate my homework,' and as we dash our hands on camera, he adds, 'but it is so, so good to see you.' He doesn't single me out, he doesn't tell us if he is married, but he does say, repeating himself, that he is happy to see us.

For years they entreated me to marry.

'It's not just for the children, you know, Niharika,' they told me, 'It's for companionship too.'

So much of the pressure was piled on by distant family and those who didn't lay a claim to love—ageing acquaintances, who would emerge at every occasion, every wedding and every festival, every evening walk even once a girl had reached the age of winsomeness—twenty if you were lucky, but often sixteen or seventeen. Contacts would be compared, eligible boys of the right family and social standing would be mentioned, and the ritual of matchmaking would commence.

Any girl with alternative plans; an education, a career, a varying sexual orientation, would be hammered with repeated proposals until she either succumbed or aged, at which point all entreaties would stop. This latter tended to coincide with the onset of the fourth decade of life, by which point a woman's eggs would have degraded, and she would be relegated firmly to the marriage trash heap. No one would ever again ask her about her plans for marriage.

A couple of days after the Zoom call, I get an email from Pranav.

The dog, he writes, did not eat my homework, but it was good to see you.

It was good to see you too.

He asks me if I still live in the neighbourhood near the DLF mall. He doesn't ask if I'm married. I don't ask him where he lives or if he's married, and he doesn't offer the information up either. He asks for my number and sends me a WhatsApp: *God, it was so nice to see you. The things you don't think you miss.*

Good to know I'm a thing.

Thing, person, schoolmate, colleague, friend, he writes back. *You take your pick.*

I tell him I haven't ventured out since March. I tell him I haven't been to the market. I tell him I haven't let the cleaning woman back in even though I continue to pay her—you can't trust public transport, and I can't vouch for the conditions she lives in at home. I tell him I miss my noisy, chaotic in-person classes, and hate seeing my little tots in little squares on a screen for their online lessons. I tell him I haven't had food delivered since March, and when I tell him I miss eating out, the relief from the drudgery of planning and cooking and ladling out and cleaning, he tells me he met a friend for a meal the weekend before.

Abhay, do you remember? He was in my section.

I don't remember him, I tell him.

He's married now, Pranav tells me, and my heart throbs illogically. He has mentioned Abhay's marital status while saying nothing about his own. *Last weekend*, he types out, *I went to their place for dinner. We sat out in the lawn and had kebabs. We didn't hug, we didn't sit indoors. We shook hands even though his wife had us rub sanitiser on our hands straight after. And you know what?* I wait, as the top left corner of my screen tells me he is typing, *even that stilted interaction felt precious to me.*

Maybe he lives alone too. Maybe he understands, like others can't, what the true cost of the pandemic has been for those of us who are on our own.

The next time we exchange messages, he tells me that he'd like to come over to say hello.

The outside world, they say, is aching to return to normal. It's the men, most often, who feel hemmed in. Not the children, who are turning too readily to their devices, but grown men, who are beginning to find excuses, a socially distanced game of golf, a morning walk, a trip to the market, to escape from their homes. The uncle next door, who has a wholesale shop in Old Delhi, tells me he can't sit at home for the rest of his life.

'I have mouths to feed, Beta,' he tells me when I see him. 'Life has to return to normal.' I'm in the garden the day after Pranav makes his offer. I'm watering the plants, rooting out the weeds, and he is standing as he always does in the mornings, by his gate, as if about to step out and disappear into the past.

Navya sometimes passes by with her mother.

'We take the long way round to the park,' explains Mrs Singh. 'It allows us to say hello to friends. There's her best friend Deepali, who lives one street along. And,' adds Mrs Singh in a stage-whisper, as if she's sharing a secret, 'Navya never lets me pass your house without hoping she can spot her favourite teacher.'

'Well, it's a treat to see you,' I say. I mean it, even though Navya is jumping from foot to foot in her hurry to move. They have so much energy at this age, and when they were in school, I would often make them sit holding their hands in their laps so their energy could pass from one hand to the other. I hadn't expected them to believe my words when I had first spoken them, but they had been taken with the notion of their exuberance being under their control, and by and large, they would behave better and focus more when they sat as instructed.

'Niharika Ma'am,' says Navya, peering through the gaps in the railing.

'Yes, Navya?'

'Do you know I have set up a book club with Rastogi Uncle?'

'Have you, now?'

Mrs Singh chimes in. 'He's our next-door neighbour,' she explains with a smile. 'He lives in the house to our right.'

I nod. Ashima had mentioned something about a book club, and I tell the girl, 'Do you know, his daughter is my best friend?'

Her eyes go wide. 'Really?'

'Really,' I tell her. 'She and I were at school together, and we would play badminton in the park every evening.'

'Oh,' she says, and then, 'But Rastogi uncle hasn't mentioned you.' I open my mouth to reply, but she is already hurrying on, her words tripping out and running into one another as she struggles to keep pace with the fleetness of her thoughts. 'And-and what I wanted to say is that …' She pauses, biting down on her lower lip, 'is that we exchange books. Roald Dahl and Panchatantra stories and Harry Potter and so on.'

'Rastogi Uncle is reading Harry Potter?'

'Yes,' she says proudly. 'I've just lent him *The Chamber of Secrets*.'

'That's very impressive, Navya,' I say. 'I don't ever remember him reading when we were growing up.'

Navya nods earnestly. 'He *was* reluctant at first. But I think he is enjoying the book club now.' She looks at her mother, who nods. 'And anyway, what I wanted to ask is if you wanted to join our book club?'

It has rained overnight, and even though the sun is bright overhead, the weather is cooler than it has been for days. Navya is skipping again, eager for me to fall in with her plans, and eager to be on the move again, and as she nods, urging my agreement, I am tempted. We've been careful, denying ourselves so much, and there is little harm, surely, in a book club.

'A book club,' I say, and she nods eagerly.

'Yes, Niharika ma'am,' she says. 'We call it the New New-Delhi Book Club. We post books through each other's letter boxes. Just as if they were letters!'

A stray dog wanders past, Mrs Singh pulls Navya close to her, and I can see the hazards of the journey. The dogs in the house opposite Mr Rastogi's, roaming unfettered now that humans have retreated, and the dangers of the exchange itself—a letter box touched by a careless postal worker, a man out for a walk spitting on the footpath, a local worker passing by too close. No, I think to myself. It's too much of a risk. I smile at Navya, and say apologetically, 'I'll be there in spirit, Navya, but school work will keep me too busy.'

'Maybe you could come over on a weekend?'

'Navya,' says her mother.

'No, no,' I tell Mrs Singh, 'it's a lovely idea. The New New-Delhi Book Club. You must keep me updated on all the books the two of you exchange.'

Mrs Singh nods, but Navya is tripping off towards her best friend's house, and she runs to catch up with her child.

Pranav mentions a day. He's passing by the area anyway, and even though I don't ask him what business he has near my home, I put some effort into my outfit. I wear a white Anarkali kurti and my oxidised silver hoops, lining my eyes with kohl and putting on the berry lip stain I had applied when we had our Zoom call.

Delhi grows warmer, the starch in my kurta wilts, and I tell myself I shouldn't expect him. There was no definite confirmation. But then my bell rings, and even though I try to shield myself from disappointment by thinking it is the Amazon parcel I ordered, or Navya on the way to the park, I straighten my clothes out as I walk to the gate.

There he is, leaning lazily against the wall. His hair no longer flops over his forehead, and instead it is thinning and is combed back over his head. He wears a white shirt he doesn't tuck into his light blue jeans, and I smile as I notice he has rolled his sleeves up to his elbow.

He's looking at me too, taking in the changes in my appearance, and as he notices me observing him, he holds out his hand. 'I have supplies,' he smiles. 'So if you do agree to shake my hand, I can give you hand sanitiser afterwards.'

I laugh as I consider his proposition. It grows hotter, my cheeks burn, and as the uncle next door opens the door of his house, I extend my hand. Pranav grabs it, shaking it, squeezing it, and I find myself smiling.

The uncle is peering at us now, frowning. His head is tilted to one side, and he is blinking rapidly, as if trying to rouse himself, and I look away. I catch my visitor's eye and shrug. He's smiling at me, his hand still in mine, and I understand what Pranav said about the joy of a physical meeting. I don't invite him in, and as we stand making our self-conscious conversation in full view of the neighbourhood, I see that even this stilted contact feels—no, is—so very precious to me.

Acknowledgements

This book owes so much to the memory of those first strange, terrifying months of lockdown in 2020, and my own images are essentially coloured by interactions with others living through the time. There are many dues in this regard, but particular thanks are owed to Rajiv Dogra, Vicky Singh, Shuchika Rajpal, Shruti Nangia and Veena Nabar for giving me glimpses of their lives in lockdown. My thanks also to my daughter, Anaia, for giving me 'How to Spoil my Brother's Birthday', and to my son, Maanas, for writing 'The Coronavirus Rhapsody' for the eponymous story. My continuing gratitude to my husband, Amarendra, for patiently reading every draft I write, and for sticking to his feedback regardless of how it is received. A previous version of 'Half a Life' appeared in Indian Literature magazine, and an earlier iteration of 'This Coronavirus Business' was published by *Adda* magazine